SINS OF THE FATHER

C. G. COOPER

"SINS OF THE FATHER"

A Corps Justice Novel
Copyright © 2017, 2018 C. G. Cooper Entertainment, LLC.
All Rights Reserved. Reproduction prohibited.
Author: C. G. Cooper

A portion of all profits from the sale of my novels goes to
fund OPERATION C4, our nonprofit initiative serving
young military officers. For more information visit
OperationC4.com.

This novel contains violence and profanity. Readers beware.

Want to stay in the loop?
Sign Up to be the FIRST to learn about new releases.
Plus get newsletter only bonus content for FREE.
Visit cg-cooper.com for details.

Join my private reader group at TeamCGCooper.com.

To my faithful readers: thank you for allowing me to continue this awesome writing journey. I could not do this without you.

For my wife and kids. You are the sunshine of my life.
- CGC

PROLOGUE

"You want another?"

The question shook Tommy Quinn from his thoughts. "Sorry?"

The bartender pointed at the nearly empty glass. "Another one?"

"Yeah. Make it a double."

"So, the same as the last?"

He nodded and resumed staring at his ice cubes. How had it all come to this? You'd think that once you got to a certain point in your life, you'd have money, power and prestige in your own way... and that you would have had it all figured out.

The words of his high school track coach came back to him. "*Eyes on the prize, Tommy, eyes on the prize.*"

Sadistic old bastard.

He remembered how he'd run till his lungs felt like they would burst from his chest that first day on the track, and had continued hard from then on. No matter what race his coach put him in – the 100, the 400, the mile – Tommy Quinn was one of those freaks who just knew how to win.

"Eyes on the prize, Tommy, eyes on the prize."

He'd taken those words and cut his own jagged seam in the world. But had it made him happy?

What the hell *was* happy, anyway? An occasional visit to his parents? Sure, it always lifted his spirits. On a good day, he'd say those visits made him truly happy. Mom and Dad were so proud. And why not? His poor folks thought Tommy had gone and made something of himself.

For a while he had. The money was good; the missions were better.

But now...

How had it all gone so wrong?

Eyes on the prize, Tommy, eyes on the prize.

"Here you go," the bartender said, setting a white napkin and a glass half full of bourbon in front of him. Tommy nodded his thanks but got nothing in return except a waft of stale smoke from somewhere. Where? The wallpaper? He was still the only patron in the joint. It was early for drinking, and the veteran bartender kept a wary eye on Tommy since the moment the kid had stepped in.

He slid aside his empty glass for the new one and then glanced down at his gold Rolex.

Almost time.

Rather than nurse this one, he threw it down his steel-drain throat in one gulp, the taste barely registering on his numb tongue.

"Hey, y'alright?" This was the first sign of concern in the bartender's voice. Too little, too late.

"Never better, my good man, never better. But if you would be so kind as to give me my tab, I think I'll close it out now."

He handed over his company card. The bartender did his thing, probably relieved that the early-bird lush was finally taking flight. While his back was turned, and he ran the card, Tommy reached into his pocket, pulled out three $100 bills, and wrapped them in a single dollar. When the bartender returned with the receipt, Tommy crossed out the tip portion. He made sure the bartender saw him do it. He could almost feel the scowl. He slid the receipt back across the bar and then set what definitely appeared to be a couple of dollar bills on the bar. "For your trouble, my good man, for your trouble."

Then he rose, gave the proprietor a pointer finger salute from his temple, and was gone.

The Maserati's engine purred as his mind repeated that damned phrase on auto-loop. *"Eyes on the prize. Eyes on the prize."* Another glance at his watch, a present from his current employer. Tommy sniffed hard. *Almost time*. His heart raced against the blood-thickening power of the booze. Getting closer now. So close.

A single tear dropped from his left eye, followed by one from his right.

He laughed. This was the first time he'd cried in years. A man in his line of work didn't have time to cry. Pain was nothing, sadness an afterthought, but this time he allowed the tears to flow. They fed his need for something to hold on to.

Closer now, so close, he thought to himself. *Don't die a sinner, Tommy*.

He revved the engine once, put the sucker in gear, and pressed on the gas. The Maserati leapt at the touch. His target appeared dead ahead. There were pedestrians on the sidewalks. Maybe they glanced his way. He didn't care. In a moment, he'd be a mere blur of a blacked-out sports car zooming by with the roar of an F-14. Besides, he knew the onlookers were safe. Even with his veins bloated with alcohol, his hands were steady on the wheel, panther eyes focused, his target looming.

Do it now, Tommy. Don't die a sinner.

His target turned. He was a man roughly Tommy's age, good looking. He was holding an ice cream cone, of all things.

Eyes on the prize, Tommy, eyes on the prize.

That last iteration made Tommy smile, the same smile he'd had when he'd run his first race, when he'd graduated from Parris Island and run into the loving embrace of his parents.

"Eyes on the prize," he muttered. Still smiling, he jerked the wheel hard to the right.

His true target, a huge tree that had probably been a sapling sometime in the 18th century, grew larger in his field of vision.

The smile never left him as he plowed headlong into the ancient relic.

CHAPTER ONE

Eight out of ten, Cal Stokes thought as he licked the ice cream he'd just purchased from the new artisanal shop on the Downtown Mall in Charlottesville. It was part of his new routine. He was trying to be more adventurous. *Be more adventurous*, he'd repeat to himself every day.

Of course, anyone who knew what Cal Stokes did for a living would laugh hearing him say this. He'd seen plenty of adventure in his lifetime. His new mantra had more to do with enjoying life and everything it had to offer, cherishing friendships and family, at least those who were left. The purchase of this eight-out-of-ten vanilla ice cream cone was another step in that journey.

He'd set a goal for himself to sample each and every one of the restaurants and shops on the Downtown Mall. The outdoor retail area had seen a resurgence in recent years. He and Diane had enjoyed many an evening strolling down the brick boulevard, arms linked, unlinking to drop so that fingers could lock together. He smiled to himself thinking about her now, as he took a sharp right and headed away from the masses, toward where he'd parked his car. It was his usual habit to walk the two miles between here and home, but there were things to do today, so he'd driven.

He was almost to the small parking lot when he heard it. It was unmistakable, the heavy revving of a luxury automobile, a purr to Cal's ears. He turned and could just make out the outline of the car coming over the crest of the hill. *Some idiot's out for a joyride*, he thought. He increased his pace to make sure he'd be out of the maniac's way. If the driver had seen him, he obviously didn't care, because he didn't slow. Cal momentarily entertained the idea of pulling the pistol from his waistband. No, that was stupid. Something you only see in action movies. You couldn't stop a car that fast with a rocket launcher, let alone a handgun. Besides, this was Charlottesville, Virginia. It was probably some college kid returning to UVA from the fall break, showing off his four-wheeled gift from Mommy and Daddy.

Someone or something was watching over Cal Stokes, because someone or something made him turn and lock eyes with the driver. The driver was intent on one thing, and one thing only: Cal Stokes.

The ice cream cone slipped from his hand. He planted his feet. Which way to run? His pulse quickened as he calculated the odds. With plenty of distance between them, he could probably get back across the street. He was fast enough for that. Or he could continue moving in the same direction he'd been going.

The driver made the decision for him.

For some reason, the kid made a hard right, and Cal's instincts kicked into overdrive. He bolted the way he'd come, turning just in time to see the Maserati plow into a massive tree, wrapping itself around it, the lightweight metal no match for solid, ancient oak. There were shouts from down the street now, and people pointing.

Cal ran to the crumpled car. By pure chance, the crash

had not completely sealed the driver's side door. With some straining, Cal pried it open, white powder from the airbag still lingering in the air like a fine mist.

A man inside, about Cal's age, the face marked with death, gray and pallid. He lolled partially out of his seat and into Cal's arms. Cal pulled at the body, but the legs were pinned in the wreckage.

"Somebody call 911!" he yelled.

It was Cal's instinct that made him scan the front seat. No weapons, at least none that he could see. Other than the gold Rolex on the man's wrist, nothing stood out as extraordinary. "Just hold on for me, ok, pal?" he said. "Help is coming. Hang in there."

Miraculously alive, the man slowly shook his head. Cal was amazed. The kid had to have been going close to 100 miles per hour when he'd hit the tree. Now that he thought about it, there was one thing out of place about this picture: the man had no seatbelt on. Somehow – by the impact, or the airbag, maybe both – he'd literally been pinned inside the car. Was this a miracle or just stupidity? Mingled with the smell of mangled metal and copper blood, Cal thought he detected a hint of alcohol.

"Hey," Cal said, trying to keep the man's fluttering eyes from closing, "what's your name?"

The eyes popped open and locked on Cal with an intensity that Cal would later remember as almost fanatical. "Cal Stokes," the man said.

Cal shook his head. "What did you say?"

The man smiled through bloody teeth, and said in a rasping whisper, "Eyes on the prize, Cal Stokes. Eyes on the prize."

And then, as if that message was the only reason he'd been left alive, his body went limp in Cal's arms, leaving Cal to wonder what the hell had just happened.

CHAPTER TWO

I t wasn't hard finding the dead man's identity. Before the paramedics and the police arrived, Cal snapped a couple pictures of the dead man's face. And Neil Patel, the Jefferson Group's resident tech genius, provided the information.

"Name's *Thomas A. Quinn, Jr.* No social media accounts, but I found some old clippings from his high school days. It says here he went by the name of Tommy."

"Tommy, eh," said Cal. "Tommy have an address?"

"Not yet," said Patel, "but I do have his parents' address, if that helps."

"It's a start."

He thought about telling the others about what had happened, but it might just turn out to be nothing. Maybe Tommy was just a guy from the Marine Corps. Cal had met too many people over the years to remember them all by face, let alone by name. So, once he'd confirmed with Neil that the police had been out to the Quinn house to inform them of their son's death, he decided that the next day he would make the drive to see Tommy's parents. Mr. and Mrs. Thomas A. Quinn, Sr's home was in Roanoke, about a two-hour drive from Charlottesville. Luckily, other than the questioning from the police, Cal's day was free.

The next morning, he met Diane at the door, just as she was returning from the gym.

"Where are you going?" she asked, pecking him on the cheek, but avoiding the full-on hug since she was drenched in sweat. It did little to tarnish her beauty. In fact, it may have even enhanced it. His heart still did that little skip thing whenever she entered the room.

"I thought I'd go visit the parents of that guy who died yesterday. You know, offer my condolences."

He felt a little guilty about not telling his girlfriend the whole story the night before, only that he'd been at the scene of the accident. She'd only worry if she knew. There'd been plenty to worry about during the last year. No need piling one more thing on top of the heap of their complicated lives. She was just starting out as an officer for Naval Intelligence, having completed her final training in Dam Neck. She was a mustang – a prior-enlisted seaman – and a damn good one. Cal's exploits had already gotten in her way once before. The last thing he wanted was to have it happen again.

But now here she was, staring at him the way she did, head cocked slightly to one side, analyzing him. She was nothing if not intuitive.

"I can come with you," she said. "I don't have much to do today."

"Don't worry about it. It shouldn't take long."

"Is Daniel going with you?" It was meant as a probe.

"No, he's busy."

He grabbed his car keys and wallet and shoved them in his pocket, trying to get out the door, but she pressed on.

"When was the last time you went out of town without Daniel?"

"Come on, Diane. I just want to make sure they're okay."

After another long stare, using nothing more than her eyes to pry the truth from beneath his layers, she smiled and said, "Okay, then I'll come with you."

"You really don't have to do that," he said quickly.

"No, it's fine. Give me five minutes. Let me shower and I'll do my makeup in the car."

There was no use arguing. She was already headed toward the bathroom and he couldn't help thinking that he should have left ten minutes earlier.

The Quinn household was easy to find. Located in one of those ranch home communities where the roads had been designed wide and spacious, plenty of room for kids to learn to ride their bikes and couples to stroll on daily walks. It was a neighborhood you'd see in an article about The Ten Best Places to Raise a Family. The leaves were mostly gone now, but some of the trees still clung to their burnt orange decor. The Quinn's house was a simple affair. An old mailbox had "Quinn" painted on the side of it in faded flowery lettering.

As he and Diane got out of the car, Cal noticed the mailbox was overflowing. He went to it and emptied its contents. Mostly junk mail, but he recognized the angry red stamps on some of the envelopes indicating overdue notices. Looking around the place, he saw some of the more subtle signs of financial struggle. Grass a little more overgrown here than on neighboring lawns. Gutters overflowing with leaves, whereas everyone else on the street had already cleaned theirs out. When they reached the door, a pile of soggy newspapers lay to one side, brushed there by repeated sweeps of the screen door.

He rang the doorbell. It was a few moments before he saw shadows moving within. A light clicked on, and a haggard face appeared in the window. The graying woman's eyes were swollen. She had a Kleenex in her hand when she opened the door. The smell of home cooking, pot roast maybe, emanated from somewhere inside.

"May I help you?" Her voice trembled, and not with age.

"Yes, ma'am. My name is Cal Stokes, and this is Diane Mayer."

No recognition that she knew the name. Not even a hand extended.

"Ma'am, I was there when your son died."

The Kleenex went to the woman's mouth. "Oh, God. You knew my Tommy?"

This was the tricky part.

"Ma'am, is your husband in? Maybe we can come inside and talk. Or we could talk outside if you prefer."

"Tom," Mrs. Quinn called to the back.

Thomas Quinn, Sr. emerged from behind her in a gray and black flannel shirt tucked in on one side. His hair was perfectly combed, but there was about a week's worth of stubble on his face.

"Who is it, Patty?" His voice was weary, like one who's been up all night.

"They say they knew Tommy."

The old man's eyes brightened at that, and before Cal could correct her, Mr. Quinn had his hand extended. "Any friend of Tommy's is welcome in our home." He seemed on the verge of tears, and not for the first time today. Cal shook the gentle hand.

The old man pulled him into the house. "Please, please, what can we get you? Coffee? Is it too late for coffee?"

Cal couldn't find the words so it was Diane who answered for them. "Coffee would be fine, please. He'll take his black and I'd like mine with a little bit of creamer, if you have it."

So they entered the Quinn home like old friends. Mr. Quinn guided Cal inside, and Mrs. Quinn followed with Diane. The place was dark. Things were tidy, like they'd been placed and not used for a long time, and as a result, a year's worth of dust lay on every surface. But that aspect changed when they walked into the kitchen. Pots and casserole dishes lined up neatly on the counter top. A slow cooker, the source of the delicious aroma of home cooking, bubbled away on one side. Pot roast, Cal confirmed. Then in the corner, Cal recognized a familiar sight, a small fold out table, one of those 1950s relics with a Formica top and a metal strip edge all around. His parents had had two just like it that they'd bring out whenever company came over. On the top of this table was an assortment of trophies, mostly track, but there was the old T-ball trophy and one that happily displayed third place in a fourth-grade soccer tournament. And right there in the center of it all, like an object of devotion, was the picture of the man he didn't know, Tommy Quinn, grinning from ear to ear and flanked by his parents at his boot camp graduation.

Mrs. Quinn let go of Diane's arm, walked over to the table, and touched the picture as if part of some ritual. "He was such a handsome boy." She stood there for a long minute, stroking the picture, and then her body shuddered and she turned to them. "Oh my, where are my manners? You said black and you said a little bit of creamer. Was that right?"

"Yes ma'am," Cal said. "Thank you."

"It's been a... busy day," Mr. Quinn said, sliding into one of the kitchen chairs. "Patty's been at it since two this morning getting the food ready for visitors. I wish we could all go back to that day," he said, pointing to the picture of his son. "We were so proud of him. He was too. He was just a weekend warrior. Do you know what that means?"

"Yes sir. I was in the Marine Corps too."

"Ah, so, is that how you knew Tommy?"

"Well, not exactly."

Unaware of the awkwardness in Cal's tone, Mr. Quinn continued. "He had done his time in the Reserves and said he wanted to go full time. He had aspirations of working for the CIA, if you can believe that." He said it in a tone filled with wonder, as if no one before Tommy had ever had the necessary skills or talent to work for the CIA.

Mrs. Quinn returned with their coffee.

"Thank you, ma'am," said Diane.

"Please, call me Patty," she said through a sniffle.

"Thank you, Patty." Diane sipped her coffee. "This is delicious."

"My family used to own a diner in Clarksdale, Mississippi. My grandmother taught me exactly how to make it, just like Daddy liked."

Diane was right. Cal had had his fair share of coffee over the years and this was the best he'd ever tasted. Then something in his gut twitched. Whether it was the caffeine hitting his brain or the guilt that he felt about lying, something forced him to come clean.

"Mr. and Mrs. Quinn," he started.

"Please," said Mr. Quinn, a tired smile on his face, "I'm Tom and she's Patty."

"Yes, sir. Well, I don't exactly know how to say this, but I didn't really know your son. The first time we met was yesterday when I tried to help him."

Patty stepped closer. "You tried to help our Tommy?"

The image of the accident flashed in his mind. He quickly suppressed it, lest any hint of the gruesome details should spill. No parent should hear about how their son's body couldn't be pulled from a mangled wreckage. "Yes ma'am," he said carefully. "I was there with him in his last moments."

"My Lord," Tom said. "And that's why you came here, isn't it? Did he say something? Oh, God. He said something, didn't he?" There were fresh tears in the old man's eyes now, and Patty sobbed silently with him. Diane got up and put an arm around her shuddering body.

Cal wracked his brain over how he should proceed now, mentally kicking himself for his lack of tact. He'd come looking for answers to his own questions, and now he'd dug a pitchfork into these poor peoples' wound.

So Cal Stokes did the best thing he knew to do in a situation like this: he lied. "He told me to tell you he loved you."

Tom Quinn, Sr. folded in half, face in his hands. "Oh," he moaned, "my boy."

Cal put a hand on the man's back. "I'm so sorry for your loss," he said softly, waiting for the man's grief to run out – at least for the moment – and the tears to subside until they were replenished once again. Eventually, Thomas Quinn, Sr. sat up straight, readjusted his shirt and looked up at Cal.

He took a cleansing breath. "Thank you for coming, and thank you for telling us that." His face brightened a little when he said, "Listen, will you please stay for lunch? We have plenty of food."

"Patty," said Diane, "why don't I help you with the food? I may not be quite the cook you are, but I can follow directions, and I'm pretty handy with a knife."

"I'll help too," Cal said.

They spent the rest of their day with the Quinns. Patty was the master chef in the kitchen, a storehouse of recipes in her brain. It only took her two minutes to figure out Diane's and Cal's level of skill, sweetly doling out small tasks.

While Cal was relegated to the chopping board, Diane was allowed to tend to the soup and monitor the casserole dishes. In between Patty's orders, Tom related memories of his son: of the day he learned to ride a bike out front; of his years as a high school track star. "He ran every race from the mile on down," the old man said proudly. "I don't know many kids who could do that. He'd finish one race and immediately prepare for the next. Damnedest thing."

"He had so much energy as a boy," Patty interjected.

"Track was a blessing. It kept both his body *and* his mind occupied."

Tom nodded. "Then, as Tommy always did, he surprised us once again. He asked us if he could enlist in the Marine Corps. Just in the reserves, of course, so he could go to college. He got a full ride to Virginia Tech to run track. He was destined for great things. All American, you know. He even thought about going to the Olympics."

By this time, Cal felt like he'd known the Quinns for years. Merely a half hour before, he would have felt awkward asking about Tommy's life. Now, there wasn't the slightest bit of awkwardness in his voice when he asked, "What did Tommy do after college?"

"Oh... this and that." It was obvious Tom was holding something back. "He had kind of a hard time... finding his way."

"I know the feeling," Cal said.

Tom nodded. "At any rate, he did finally find a job. It paid good money too, but it kept him away a lot. We'd gotten used to seeing him at least every weekend, but now he was gone for months at a time. And it changed him somewhat. Some weekends he would come back happy. Other weekends he would come home and barely say five words to us. He said he couldn't tell us stories because it was some kind of top secret deal. He said it was security, but, well, you never know with those things. On those silent weekends, he'd hole up in his old room with a case of beer, and only come out to get more." He rubbed wearily at his forehead. "Dear God, I don't know why I didn't do anything about it. It's just as parents, you don't want to pry. Do you think he understood that?"

"I'm sure he did," Cal said honestly. "You can only do so much. It sounds like you did the best you could."

"Yes, well, sometimes your best isn't good enough, is it?"

There was a long silence, with only the sound of bubbling soup filling the void.

"You know," Cal said, "I lost both of my parents on 9/11." He felt uneasy in this rare instance of letting someone in. But he'd done it, and then realized he didn't regret it.

"Oh, I'm so sorry to hear that," Patty said. "And here we are going on and on about Tommy—"

"No, it's fine, really, " Cal said. "I don't even know why I brought it up. I guess I just wanted you know that I understand the grief you must be feeling right now. I remember how I didn't have anyone to talk to. At least that's what I thought. I ran to the Marine Corps and they accepted me with open arms. But it didn't change the fact that I was in a lot of pain for a long time. And now, I can only imagine the pain that results from having lost a son." The words were coming freely now. These were closely guarded emotions, he realized. Rarely had he shown them to anyone but his closest friends. Even then, he still measured them out carefully. But now, in the tiny kitchen, surrounded by grief and memories of the past, he found he couldn't help but share *his* grief. He told them about how he'd left school and gone to boot camp, isolating himself, ignoring every person who tried to contact him. He told them of the message his father had left moments before Flight 77 became a human torpedo and crashed into the Pentagon. Then he told them about the peace that he'd found when he realized that his parents were always looking down on him.

"It took a long time," he said, his voice wracked with the pain of memory. "I won't lie. They were good people and even better parents. They loved me unconditionally, even when *I* was the handful. My father had gotten out of the Marine Corps because of me. He told me he'd done it so he'd never miss another moment. I never doubted their love. I guess that's what made it that much harder. That love."

He felt Diane's rapt gaze upon him, knowing that she'd never been witness to this layer of Cal Stokes. He cleared his throat, the raw emotion of the day threatening to overtake him. "I guess what I'm trying to say is if you need someone to talk to, you're more than welcome to call me."

Tom extended his hand. "Thank you, son. I appreciate that."

Cal accepted the man's hand gratefully. He decided he wouldn't press these people. He wouldn't ask what they thought the connection was. Not now. Perhaps there would be time for that later, but for now, his heart settled in knowing that he, Cal Stokes, might be able to provide a small measure of solace for two people in pain. In that moment, he coined a phrase for himself:

The loving embrace of a stranger is better than no embrace at all.

CHAPTER THREE

Cal and Diane didn't say much on the drive back to Charlottesville. They relegated themselves to listening to a Top 40 station, each lost in their thoughts. By the time they'd gotten home, Cal was convinced that it all had been some strange coincidence - that Tommy Quinn had somehow recognized him from their time in the Marine Corps; that there was no conspiracy, and that the wreck had just been the tragic end in a troubled man's life.

"Thanks for going with me," he said as they were about to get out of the car. Diane squeezed his hand and said nothing. Now he really wanted to explain everything to her. She knew he was holding something back, and he knew that she knew it. But the grief of the day made talking about it impossible. Any conversation would only dig up bad memories.

"How about I order us some dinner?" Cal suggested, when they'd entered their rented home.

"I'm not really that hungry." She slipped out of her coat and hung it behind the door.

"Yeah, me neither."

For a moment he stood there, unsure of what to say. Would she call him out on his lie, here, now?

"I'm sorry about your parents," she said.

He nodded. Of course they'd talked about his parents before, but never to the degree he'd talked about them today.

She stepped closer. "Cal, I'm serious. I'm so sorry. I can't imagine what you've gone through."

The reply he wanted to make was trapped behind the lump in his throat. He reached out and stroked her cheek. She touched his hand gently, and that was all it took. They came together like magnets, their love for each other, the pain of lost ones, and the joy of being alive and together finally unleashed in a torrent of raw physicality. Their lips locked. And he picked her up and carried her to the bedroom.

The buzzing of his phone on the bedside table came just after 2:30 in the morning. Woozily, he picked it up and squinted at the screen. At first he didn't recognize the phone number. Then it hit him. It was Tom Quinn.

"Tom, is everything okay?" he said quietly.

"Cal?" The old man sounded worried.

"Yeah, it's me."

"I'm sorry to call so early but, well, I hate to impose." A pause, then, "Could you come here?"

"Of course," he said without hesitation. "I'll leave in five minutes." There were muffled voices in the background – maybe Mrs. Quinn, but with other male voices commingled. "Tom, is everything okay?"

"It is now, but, if you could hurry I would appreciate it."

The call ended. He rose quickly from the bed.

"Everything okay?" Diane asked groggily.

"That was Tom Quinn. I've got to go."

"Wait," she said, "what?"

"Something's happened. I'm not sure what."

She'd snapped wide awake. "Let me come with you."

"No, you've got that thing for work today."

"At least call Daniel," she said, her head falling back onto the pillow.

Before, it had been as easy as walking down the hall and knocking on Daniel Briggs's door, but Cal and Diane had decided to rent a house a few blocks from The Jefferson Group's headquarters, which Diane called The Frat House. Even though the house was spotless, it was still constantly buzzing with the Jefferson Group's warriors, most of whom either lived there or in the auxiliary house across the street.

He dressed quickly, texting Daniel as he slipped on his shoes. As usual, Daniel texted right back and said he'd be out front in five minutes. He was there in four, no questions asked.

To his friend, Cal opened up entirely, explaining everything to Daniel in detail, from the crash, to Tommy Quinn's final words and, of course, the phone call from Tom Quinn, Sr. Daniel didn't say a word while he drove.

They were an hour into their journey before he asked, "Does Diane know?"

"No," Cal said. "It could be nothing."

When they arrived at the Quinn house, they were greeted by police tape and departing squad cars. Tom Quinn came out in a brown robe and ripped down a strip of tape to let them in.

"There's been a break-in."

"Are you alright?"

"We're okay. The missus is a little shaken up. She's going to offer you coffee. Humor her, will you? The cops wouldn't take it."

They followed him inside where a distraught Patty Quinn rose from the couch to greet them. "Oh Cal, thank you for coming. Here, let me make you some coffee. I think I have some cake too."

"That would be a pleasure," he said. "By the way, this is Daniel Briggs. Daniel Briggs, Tom and Patty Quinn."

Handshake. "How do you do, son?"

"Daniel's an old, trusted friend."

With the introductions out of the way, the sniper disappeared, already seeking out the scent. By means of distraction, Cal said, "Let's see if we can't talk some sense into your lovely wife," and took Tom into the kitchen.

"Patty, don't you think you ought to go to bed?"

She looked at him like he was crazy. Who would make the coffee?

"You're safe now," said her husband.

"And you need sleep," Cal said, leaning an elbow on the fridge.

Patty fiddled with the coffee basket, trying to separate two stuck-together filters. "I guess, but I don't know."

"Is it the coffee?" Cal said. "I think it'll brew just fine without you. With all due respect."

She gave him a trusting smile. Passing him, she gave him a gentle pat on the cheek, then kissed her husband goodnight.

Stopping at the kitchen threshold, she turned. "That man in there. Is he...?"

"He's fine," Cal said with a smile. "I trust him with my life."

She returned his smile with hers, a warm smile full of years.

Cal and Tom then sat down at the table.

"Talk to me. What happened?"

The old man's voice was monotone, almost robotic. Cal surmised this was at least the third time he'd recounted the story tonight. He marveled at the man's toughness, evidenced by the fact he still had energy to speak.

"Well, let's just say it's a good thing I'm at that age where I have to get up to pee every two hours. I'd just gone to the bathroom when I thought I heard something. Patty was still asleep. Figured maybe it was my old ears playing tricks on me. Now, there's never been a robbery in all the years we've lived in this neighborhood, but I still always sleep with my pistol under the nightstand. Something told me it'd be a good idea to grab my weapon before going to investigate. I padded out into the hallway and there he was, black ski mask and all, right out of Central Casting. I didn't hesitate. I shot, but my round went high." He gestured with his hand over his head. "*Shoom!* Right out there. The police already dug out the nine millimeter slug and took it with them. Don't know what good it'll do, of course. Well, that's all it took. The guy in the mask went right out the front door. Slipped out more than ran. Disappeared before I could get a better look at him. And that was it. Whole thing took no more than 20 seconds."

The old man worked his jaw, his tongue darting out to moisten his dry lips. He was obviously still replaying the scene in his head. Cal gave him a moment and then asked, "Tom, I was just wondering why you called me. Don't get me wrong, I'm happy to be here, but I'm not sure what I can do."

For a brief moment, he wondered if Tom knew what he did for a living.

"I'm a pretty good judge of character, Cal. I knew something was wrong with my son. He wasn't right. Tommy tried to be calm, but I could see it was all an act. There was something bubbling under the surface, never letting him sit still. Then there's you. When we met yesterday I could tell that you were a good man. I saw how you were with Diane, and I can't tell you how much it meant that you spent the day with us. So, when I got back to the bedroom and saw your phone number, it just seemed right that I call, after I called the police, of course. At any rate, as I'm sure you know, we're kind of alone in the world, Tommy being... gone and all. Most of our old friends have moved out of the neighborhood. Lots of nice young couples now, but it's pretty much just Patty and me. I hope you don't mind that I called."

"Of course not. Like I said, I'm happy to be here."

The old man seemed to be chewing on a phrase. "Cal, there's one other thing. Something I told the police, but they didn't really seem to hear me."

"What is it?"

"Well I-, I know the police officers think it's just one of those smash and grab type things, you know, that the guy was probably here for money or maybe some jewelry, but I had my wallet sitting right there at the kitchen table, even had the car keys right next to it. No way the guy missed it. But he never touched them." He stopped abruptly and shook his head. "I'm sorry, never mind. I'm overthinking it. I probably just got lucky, got the jump on him, you know?"

"Listen," said Cal, "would you mind if I took a look around, see if maybe the police missed anything?"

The old man grinned. "That's what I was hoping you'd do."

"Well then, how's about this. It's only two or three hours until daylight. Why don't you go to bed now, see if you can't get a little rest. We'll hang around until daylight and make plans from there. Sound good?"

Relief spread across the man's face, like the burden had finally lifted. "Thank you, son. I really mean that. Thank you."

Cal rose and put a hand on the man's shoulder. "Everything's going to be all right, Tom."

His words had all the comfort he'd meant for them to have, but he still couldn't help the feeling that crept beneath his skin. It told him that this seemingly petty burglary was merely the first act in a much longer drama.

CHAPTER FOUR

Senator Warren Fowler gazed out the huge bay window to the snow covered fields of the early Wisconsin winter. While most hated the frigid temperatures of his home state, Senator Fowler relished the crisp bite of the cold weather. It made him feel alive. Even in his early 70s, he enjoyed cross-country skiing and the occasional snowshoe jaunt with his dogs.

If only there was time for that today. Ever since the presidential election, his schedule overflowed, as a recently-picked chairman of the Republican National Committee's schedule should. The former senator from Wisconsin was in the thick of it all. The Republicans had lost the election, and this fact had come as no surprise to the senator or his colleagues on the right. The new president, Brandon Zimmer, a Democrat from Massachusetts, was a good man, a solid leader, and in many ways more Republican than some of Fowler's own colleagues.

But it wasn't Zimmer's good standing that had won the election.

It had been the actions of his opponent, a rising star in

the Republican Party. With Zimmer's popularity soaring, Congressman Antonio McKnight was the only man who could compete with him at the time.

It had been impossible to keep all the details from leaking to the public. Congressman McKnight had done the unthinkable. Just prior to their first televised debate, McKnight had attacked the President of the United States with a knife. A brief scuffle ensued and Zimmer, after being stabbed multiple times by McKnight, somehow summoned the strength to toss his attacker off a wooden balustrade and down to his death.

The White House, the Secret Service, and a few in the know had come to the awful realization that the congressman's actions could not be swept under the rug. They fashioned his story out of whole cloth: Congressman McKnight was a troubled soul and had hidden his demons well. Fowler was one of a dozen who knew the truth: that the Miami-bred McKnight was a sociopath who'd transformed scraps of a ruined childhood into a win-at-all-costs machine; and that it was only through sheer cunning that this man without a conscience had reached the highest heights of the Washington elite.

He had to tip his hat to a man like that. Such ambition, such strength to do it all on his own. There were details even he would never find out. Details that only the Secret Service and the president knew. Darker secrets. Things that should never be allowed to see the light of day. Senator Warren Fowler knew about such secrets. He had his own.

There was a knock on the door.

"Come in," Fowler said.

A young man marched in, mouth already open to give his report.

Fowler held up a hand. "Is it cold in here?"

The man took his meaning and pulled out the cell phone from his pocket.

The senator's bodyguard emerged from a shadowed corner of the room, grabbed the phone, and set about frisking the visitor.

"I'm sorry about all this cloak and dagger nonsense," Fowler said, congenially. "Cigar?"

The younger man nodded as he took a seat in front of Fowler's desk. Fowler selected two Maduros from his humidor, handing one to the man. As the thick smoke billowed above, Fowler asked "Do you remember Operation Mantis?"

The young apprentice froze, then licked his lips. "Yes, sir. I remember." He looked like he was about to choke on the cigar smoke still in his lungs. He even coughed a little bit out.

"As it turns out, we've had a breach."

The young man went from gray to green. Fowler's gaze went from fatherly kind to icy cold.

"Relax," said Fowler. "If I'd wanted you dead, I wouldn't have wasted a cigar on you." The lightness in his voice returned. "Are you okay? You look a little peaked."

"Just woozy from the cigar," the man said quickly. "This is a good one, Senator. Cuban?"

Fowler snorted, as if a senator from Wisconsin would even think about smoking one of those Communist sticks. "Dominican. But, while I'd love to chat about cigars, that's not why I summoned you here. I want you to interview your staff. Find the leak and report it to me."

"Senator, I-"

"Just find it," Fowler snapped, but he kept his smile warm. It's the same one that had won over thousands of voters over the years. The man even the media had taken to calling "Uncle Warren" for his warm disposition turned back to the window, puffing his cigar. It was a dismissal and the man knew it. Fowler didn't speak again until the man was gone.

The shadowy figure from the corner emerged once more. "Do you think it was him?"

"No," Fowler answered, "but it won't hurt to keep him paranoid. I know exactly who the leak was."

"Who?"

"A dead kid," said Fowler, taking a long, slow pull from his cigar. He let it out in a thin stream that hit the window and plumed out. "A very dead kid in a very expensive car. And I'd very much like to recoup my losses. I'll have the details to you by nightfall."

The man from the shadows said nothing more, but walked back to his post in the shadows, leaving Fowler to once again calculate which way to turn the ship. It wasn't much of a decision.

For him, there was only one true North: Revenge, plain and simple.

CHAPTER FIVE

P atty Quinn put Cracker Barrel to shame.

The full spread of pancakes, French toast, eggs, and mounds of bacon left both Cal and Daniel stuffed. Tom and Patty barely touched their food. Husband and wife were not eager to see the Marines leave, so Daniel Briggs did what he always did: he made things happen. A couple of phone calls and within fifteen minutes, a police cruiser was sitting out front. Daniel had a few words with the police officer and was assured that the Quinns would be watched night and day.

"Again," said Tom, "we can't thank you enough."

"No need," said Cal. "Give me a call if you need anything. Anything at all."

"Let me at least pay for your gas. Will you let me do that?"

Cal chuckled genially. "Your hospitality was more than enough."

"I feel like we're imposing on your life," Tom said.

"You're family now," Cal replied, surprised that he really meant it. "I like to take care of family. Daniel doesn't say much, but trust me, he's the exact same way. So, like I said, if you need anything, call me."

With soft eyes, Tom smiled and nodded, then went back into the house with his wife.

Daniel waved to the cop at the curb as they pulled away.

"Do you think we should get them a place to stay, at least until this blows over?" Cal asked his friend.

"I think they'll be okay with the police for now. Maybe it is all just a coincidence," Daniel said.

They'd already discussed the break-in while the Quinns had slept, and ran over it again now. Whoever had gotten in was good. No sign of forced entry. According to the Quinns, nothing had been taken, but from careful analysis, Daniel had detected that a couple pieces on the mantle and on the living room coffee table had been moved around. The thick collection of dust told that story.

They were winding their way through town, headed back towards the highway, when Daniel said, "We're being followed. Maroon Ford Ranger. Four cars behind. One man in the cab."

Cal didn't have to look. If anyone could sniff out a tail, it was Daniel Briggs. "Since when?"

"Just after we left the neighborhood."

"See if you can bring them in close. I want a better look."

"You got it."

So instead of making their way back to the interstate, Daniel took a circuitous route, meandering in and out of morning traffic.

Once they were one hundred percent sure that they were being followed, Cal said, "He's not making much of an effort to stay hidden. Make your way to the highway. Let's see where we can take this."

Daniel did as instructed and turned left. Suddenly they

were out of the morning logjam. Sure enough, a few cars later, their pursuer followed.

"We'll take him at the on-ramp. You ready?"

It was a silly question. When was Daniel not ready?

The truck was gaining on them. Daniel slowed just enough to let the cars behind get close. Soon it was their car, a sedan, and the truck behind that.

Daniel's timing was perfect. He jammed on the gas and then slammed on the brake as if the engine had locked up on itself. By now the maroon pickup was sandwiched from behind with nowhere else to go. Cal made his move, bolting from the car. He caught a quick eye of the driver in the maroon truck. Mid to late twenties. Narrow eyes. Blue ball cap.

No sooner than he eyed him, the driver bolted from the cab and headed toward the highway and the steep embankment leading down to the four lane road.

The guy was quick. Cal felt the buzz of adrenaline in his veins as he amped up his pursuit.

Just as his quarry hit the lip of the hill, Cal dove, slamming into the man's back. Over and over they tumbled, neither man gaining the upper hand. Cal's hip slammed into something hard. He tried to grab hold of the man. End over end they went, until they were at the bottom of the hill.

The man hopped to his feet first, seemingly no worse for wear. Cal hopped up a split second later, too late to block the haymaker that clipped him in the left side of the face. He rolled with it, taking some of the pain, and feeling his head swim, but he'd taken worse hits before. The hit was hard, but would have been harder if his own reflexes hadn't been as fast. He finished his roll on one knee, bracing himself for a hand-to-hand match, but the guy was off and running again.

It was then that a black motorcycle swerved out of traffic

and pulled off to the shoulder. The man in the blue cap hopped on. Before Cal was to his feet, they'd sped off.

He rubbed his jaw and his hip. At least now he was sure: the thing with the Quinns wasn't a coincidence. It was no use second guessing what he'd done just now. He'd seen an opportunity and taken it. Perhaps he could have shot the man, but on what grounds? A hunch? And besides, the last thing Cal wanted to have to do was explain to the cops why he'd killed a man in cold blood. The Jefferson Group was made up of elite warriors who worked directly for the president, but even *they* weren't above the law when it came to working in the public eye.

Cal straightened his shirt and did a quick canvas of the area in a vain attempt to salvage something from the situation. About ten feet away, there it was in the grass: a piece of metal that didn't belong. When he reached down to pick it up, he realized it wasn't metal. It just had a glossy sheen. It was rectangular, about the size of a wallet or a passport holder. He turned it over in his hands. There was a zipper around the seam. Unzipping it, his eyes narrowed at what he saw. Inside was a stack of mini photos, the size kids get when they have pictures done for their yearbook. The picture on top was of Tom Quinn Sr. in his bathrobe going to get the mail. The second was of Patty looking out the window.

But what really made Cal's jaw clench was the next picture. It was an image of himself, from days before, squatting next to a wrecked Maserati, cradling the lifeless body of Tommy Quinn.

CHAPTER SIX

Something about the Georgetown bar always reminded Master Sergeant Willy Trent of the movie The Firm. "Top", as the former Marine Master Sergeant was called by his friends, could just see the young Tom Cruise playing Mitch McDeere, prowling the place as a law student, shuttling pizza, and as a newly minted member of the firm with ties to the mob. The upscale pub had that kind of intrigue. Students mingled with politicians. Money men sipped on martinis while college athletes downed pitchers of beer. It was a lively place with an unwritten rule: You never got in a fight at Hanrahan's.

He'd come in for a drink and to watch the game. But at some point, he'd shifted his attention away from the TV. Another kind of drama was being played out at the other end of the bar. A guy in a suit, tie pulled down to his third button, talking the ear off of a girl who was saying nothing, but nodding politely every once in a while. To Top's trained eye, it was clear that she was uncomfortable. The date, if that's what he was, kept buying drinks and the girl kept refusing.

Top looked around. Nobody else seemed to take notice, or care. But he knew what he was looking at. It was something about the body language. With every inch the guy moved to get closer, the girl inched away. Soon there was nowhere else for her to go.

Top downed his drink and stood. His near seven-foot frame towered above the rest of the crowd. Despite his size, he weaved his way effortlessly through the packed crowd until he was standing right behind the couple that had caught his interest.

"Excuse me, miss," he said to the girl. That cut off the date's jabbering, and they both looked up at him in surprise. Top registered disgust on the man's face, which quickly turned to feigned congeniality when he saw the size of the man looming behind. "I'm sorry miss, but I think I know you. I went to school with your father. You were about this high back then." Top motioned to his waist, and ever so subtly, so only she could see, he winked. She instantly got his meaning.

"Oh yes, I'm so sorry. I didn't recognize you," she said, extending her hand.

"Yes, ma'am. The name's Willie Trent."

"I'm Mary."

"That's right. How rude of me. How could I forget such a pretty name? How is your father these days?"

"Oh, he's fine," she said. She was a gifted actress.

"Hey, look, man," the date said. "We were having a conversation. Do you mind?"

"I don't mean to be rude, but it seemed kind of like a one-way conversation."

"We're on a date," the date said, doing his best to salvage his pride. He was full of liquored courage, his words starting to slur.

"Well, Mary, I didn't mean to butt in. You know us old-timers."

"Oh, no, that's okay," Mary said quickly. "I was just leaving."

She went to rise, but her date grabbed her by the wrist. "We just got here," he said angrily. He wasn't completely stupid, as he realized what he'd done and quickly let go of Mary's wrist. "Come on. Just a couple more drinks. You said you liked this place."

"Mary, would you like me to call you a cab?" Top asked.

The date didn't give Mary a chance to reply. "Hey, Grandpa, why don't you beat it?"

Top winked at Mary again, just to let her know that everything was all right. She was tense. And boy wonder was just plain stupid.

"Oh, I'll take off," Top said, said turning to the boy, "But first, you mind if I show you a bar trick?" He didn't wait for the clown to answer as he reached into his pocket and pulled out a single dollar bill. The date glanced furtively at the twisting bill in Top's hand. "I heard a story once of this guy, a young kid, just like you. You see, this guy met a girl. The only problem was that they lived on opposite sides of the country. So what does this guy do? He decides to take a trip. He jumps in his car and just starts driving. Now, back then, he didn't have some fancy phone that could tell him the weather. The snow started falling hard. But, on he plowed. And the snow fell and the ice slicked the roads. The highways were clogged from the mess so he took out an old paper map and went the back way, over steep hills and black ice roads. He ignored all the signs and just kept driving, thinking about that girl. You see, he really, really, *really* wanted to see that girl.

"On he went through the night. Somehow, he made it through a couple of states. Dumb luck, I guess. The storm still raged, but the poor guy ignored it. He thought he was safe in that car, safe in the memory of that pretty girl. He got tunnel vision, you see. Well, at some point, the weather just got too bad. I'll spare you the details, but that fine young man swerved and skidded off the road, crashed, and died right there in the middle of nowhere. But here's the kicker. He didn't die right away. They say he lay there for hours, pinned against the wheel with broken ribs and who knows what else. He was barely able to breathe, and probably died thinking about that girl."

By now, Top had twisted the dollar bill into a tight cone with a pointy end. He held it up for a moment and admired it.

"What's your point?" the date asked with a huff.

"My point, sir, was that this poor young man failed to see the signs. He failed to see that he was walking into something he could not handle. He had never once driven in snow. He had never once driven more than 100 miles at one time. He was in uncharted territory, but he was young, and he felt invincible, and the thought of that girl kept him going."

The date snorted. "You're crazy, you know that?"

"Oh, I've heard that before, but I'll tell you what. You see this little dollar bill on my finger?" Top held it up so the man could see. "You know if you fold a newspaper this way you can kill a man with it? Yeah, yeah, I know what you're thinking. No way, right? But I've seen it. Now, I've got a bet with an old friend. I told him I thought you could probably do the same thing with a dollar bill. That's sturdy paper they make those dollar bills with. Gotta be sturdy to pass between all those hands. All you've gotta do is shove it right up here." Top showed him the spot right under his jawline. "So yeah, I've got this bet, and well, I've got nothing but time."

Then, as if he'd remembered his manners, Top jammed the dollar bill back in his pocket. "But like I said, I'm so sorry I interrupted. Mary, it was a pleasure to see you again," and then he pointed to the other end of the bar. "I'll be right over there if you need me. And, sir," he said to the date, clapping him on the back hard, "It was a pleasure to meet you as well." He gave the boy one final grin and then returned to his perch across the way.

No sooner had he gotten there when his phone beeped. Before he could type a reply to the text, Mary was right next to him. Top glanced back to where she and her date had been. He was gone.

"I just wanted to say thank you, Mr. Trent," she said nervously. "I met him online and he seemed so nice, but when he showed up, he was already drunk."

"That's all right, Mary. I'm sorry you had to go through that. How about I walk you to your car, just in case."

"My roommate dropped me off and *he*," she pointed to where her date had been, "was supposed to be my ride home."

"Well, not to worry. Modern technology shall save the day." Top pulled up the Uber app on his phone. "Well, will you look at that. There's a car right around the corner."

The girl, pleasantly shocked, said, "You don't need to do that."

"Mary, it is my treat. It is not often that I get to save the day for a young lady such as yourself."

"That's very nice of you. If you give me your phone number, I'd be happy to pay you back."

He held up a hand. "Completely unnecessary. Like I said, my treat. Now, my phone says that the car should be here in exactly one minute. Amazing this technology. How bout I walk you out and make sure you get there safe?"

Mary nodded and Top caught the eye of the bartender who slipped his tab across the bar. Laying a $50 bill on top of it, he left Hanrahan's with Mary at his side.

Once he explained to the driver that he was not coming along for the ride, he said a cordial farewell to Mary. He waved as the car drove off, then he turned back to his phone. The text had been from Cal.

Need you back in Charlottesville. Something's come up.

The Marine typed in his reply.

Sorry. I was just playing Captain America. Be home in a couple of hours.

CHAPTER SEVEN

When you've been through hard times, when you've seen death, destruction, and also their polar opposites; lives snatched from the cruel grip of the Grim Reaper, and light where there once was none, you sometimes develop a taste for peculiar trivialities. At times, this coalesces into an old habit based on an even older memory.

For Gaucho, former Delta operator and current team leader for The Jefferson Group, this took the form of waiting in lines. It didn't matter where he was, the grocery store, Disneyworld, or where he stood now, in the line at the post office. His memories loved to take him back to those early days with his mother. They would stand in line for what felt like days waiting for assistance from the church, or holding out for one more hour in the hopes of scoring some menial job.

You would think that Gaucho would hold such memories in low regard, a piece of his history that he'd like to forget, but it was in those moments of waiting that his mother would relay her patient wisdom. A native of Mexico, his mother was a gentle soul with a strict work ethic. She would tell young

Gaucho stories of the family's past, always with a lesson to be discovered within its meaning like hidden treasure. Sometimes it was as simple a lesson as "always do your best", or that in their new home, the United States, he should take care to know the land and to know the language. The most important lesson of all, however, was threefold: to be a good man, to acquire knowledge, and to never go back to the place from where they came.

Gaucho replayed those memories now, a small indulgence on his part, his mother long dead. "You always do your best, Chito," she would say in her broken English. She'd been so proud to be an American, even when she was mocked for her accent or turned away from yet another job. There was always that pride. And of course, when she'd finally gotten her American citizenship, after applying and months of studying, it had been a grand day in their little family.

Gaucho's devotion to fighting for his country meant that he'd never had time to raise a family of his own. But he had no doubt that, through his actions, he'd paid his mother's wisdom forward. Her legacy lived on through him, and through those he touched. And so, as the line at the post office shifted one more person forward, Gaucho was content, even as the man behind him grumbled something about how long it took, and the woman two ahead complained about the skyrocketing price of shipping a large envelope.

Finally, Gaucho got his turn. Now, fully flooded with the spirit of his mother, he chuckled warmly in her memory. *In a post office, of all places*, he thought, saying a quick prayer for her beloved soul.

"Good afternoon, sir. How may I help you?" said the clerk behind the high counter. She had the tired look that all civil employees acquire after one too many years on the job.

"I just have these to mail." He handed over two standard size manila envelopes.

"You know sir, there's a kiosk right outside in the lobby. You are welcome to use them at any time." She paused for a moment, apparently waiting for him to snatch them back and run to the kiosk.

He smiled and said, "Thank you. I'll keep that in mind for next time."

The clerk gave a little huff that could've indicated that for every hundred times she mentioned the self-service station, maybe one person would take her up on the offer. Gaucho could see she wasn't a bad person, just haggard, overworked. But her swift keystrokes, the efficient way she tore the postage and laid it lovingly upon the envelope, showed her skill.

When she finished, she totaled the bill and said, "How would you like to pay for that, sir?"

Before he could get out the words, "Credit, please," There was a loud bang from behind, like someone dropped a box on the floor. Gaucho did not turn like everyone else did, but he did see the eyes of the clerk go wide.

"Nobody move," came the raspy male voice. The clerk shot her hands into the air. Gaucho still didn't turn but whispered reassuringly to the clerk, "It'll be okay." A baby was crying. Someone was whimpering nearby.

"You, shorty, at the counter, turn around."

"You said not to move," Gaucho replied, staring straight ahead.

"I said, turn around."

Gaucho turned around slowly. The disheveled man hadn't even thought to wear a mask. Didn't he know that robbing a post office was a federal crime? And that maybe, possibly, there were cameras in here?

"Everyone, take out your wallets. Put them on the floor. And you, behind the counter, all the money in the bag." He tossed a backpack over Gaucho's head. Everyone was fumbling with pockets or purses as the man panned back and forth with his pistol. It took a few moments for the thief to realize that Gaucho hadn't moved.

"I said put your wallet on the floor, shorty!"

"Sorry. No can do, *amigo*."

"What did you say?" The man stepped closer, his features twisted with rage.

"I said, no can do. Lunch is on me today and the boys might get upset if I come home empty-handed."

"Listen, asshole, you and your freak show braided beard can go to hell. I will shoot you if you don't give me your money. Do you understand?"

A woman's whimper of protest came from somewhere.

"All right," Gaucho said, "you win." He slipped his wallet out of his pocket, careful not to reveal the other bulge in his waistband, and tossed it up onto the mail counter that lay between them. The man snatched it up and stuffed it in his hoodie pocket. The back and forth had given Gaucho the information he needed. All he had to do now was wait.

Confident that Gaucho was no longer a threat, the robber started barking orders to the rest of them.

"You, over there," he shouted to an old man in a wool coat, "gather up all the wallets and put them in one of those mailers." The old man did as instructed, his entire body trembling as he went about his task. The gun-wielding man turned to a mother huddled in the corner, trying her best to soothe her crying child. "And you, shut that baby up."

With the crook's focus wholly on the screaming child, Gaucho made his move.

He pivoted, and with his momentum, reached out to yank the mail scale from the counter between him and the clerk. With one fluid motion, he spun the rest of the way around and flung it at the criminal. But he didn't stop there. With a quick hop, he was on top of the tall table, even as the scale slammed into the man's gun wielding hand, sending the weapon flying, and undoubtedly shattering bones in the empty hand. The man somehow bit back the pain while his eyes followed the weapon as it skittered across the floor. Too late, he realized that another threat loomed overhead.

Gaucho timed his jump perfectly, and when he came down, the man's hands were in the air between them, trying to block him – an impossible feat. Gaucho might have been smaller in stature, but his short, burly form was more than a match for his target. Knees leading the way, he crashed into the man's chest. Legs crumpled. The man howled. A second later, the former Delta operator was straddling his prey.

"Don't move," he said to the man who was struggling to regain his breath. "Someone call the police!"

His phone was buzzing in his pocket. He pulled it out and grinned. "Hey, Cal." Gaucho listened for a moment and then said, "Sure. Let me finish what I'm doing, then I'll be on my way." He hung up the phone and then said to the wide-eyed man underneath him, "You know, you really oughta work on your timing."

CHAPTER EIGHT

Most of the Jefferson Group's key players were now in attendance. Their CEO, Jonah Layton, was out of the country with the president, and Dr. Higgins, their chief psychologist and expert interrogator, was at Fort Bragg helping the Army. They would both be apprised of the situation if it really did turn out to be a situation. Cal and Daniel had already relayed the story of the chase to Top, Gaucho, and Neil. Neil was only half-listening as he clicked away on four different computer screens.

"So," Top said, "you're sure you don't remember this Quinn kid?"

"I don't know," Cal said, "maybe. You know how it is in the Corps. I could've met him once, but it wasn't memorable enough for the name or the face to stick."

"What about his parents?" Gaucho said. "Do you think they have something to do with it?"

"No way. They're good people. I'm not sure what their son was into, but I'll bet they were trying to help him out."

"What do you mean, *help him out*?"

"Neil found out that they took out a second mortgage on

their home in the past six months. Their near-perfect credit tanked."

"I got those utilities paid, by the way," Neil said.

"What utilities?" Top asked.

"When Diane and I went to visit them the first time, there was a stack of overdue utility bills in their mailbox. I had Neil pay the bills online."

"That was nice of you."

Cal shrugged. "It wasn't much. Besides, like I said, they're good people. I'd hate to see their electricity turned off."

"Okay, so let's rehash," Top said, leaning forward. "You were out getting an ice cream cone with sprinkles on top and a Maserati crashes not fifty feet from where you stand. You go to help and the guy inside says your name and 'eyes on the prize.' What does that mean?"

"Honestly," Cal said, "maybe it was just something he said all the time. A dying man can say all sorts of things, you know that."

Everyone around the room nodded in agreement, except for Neil.

"Okay," Top continued. "So this guy dies in your arms, and you and Diane go and visit his parents. By the way, does Diane know about all of this?"

"She doesn't know *all* the details."

Top tilted his head skeptically. "You think that's smart?"

"After what happened in Europe, I'd like to know all the facts before I tell my girlfriend, if that's okay with you."

Top held up his massive hand, taking the hint.

"So look, I think we dig into this guy's life, talk to his old friends, maybe see if his Marine reserve unit remembers him."

"What about the guy that clocked you?" Gaucho asked.

It was Neil who answered. "I just got into the system at

Roanoke. They don't have cameras at that junction. So no dice on a positive I.D. "

"All we've got is Tommy Quinn," Top added.

"And his parents," Cal said.

"And his parents."

"Now," Cal said, "say we divvy up the—"

"I got it!" Neil said suddenly. He was pulling up multiple windows now, one after another, as everyone gathered around.

"Okay, here's what I've got," Neil said. "It took me longer than normal because our systems aren't completely back on line yet. I've been having to assemble it piece by piece. Modular systems are great, but they can be a bitch when you find yourself in need of a part."

"Sure, sure," said Cal. "What'd you find?" Urging his sometimes distracted friend forward was a cross he'd had to bear often.

"Well, Thomas Quinn Jr. worked for a conservative think tank in D.C. called The America Institute."

"Doesn't ring a bell. What did he do for them?"

"Let's see... it says here he was a security consultant. Got paid pretty well for it too." Then he paused, scanning the screen. "Hmmm, that's interesting... a few months back, eight to be exact, The America Institute suffered a massive cyber security breach. Everyone was put on high alert. Now that's not rare these days, but what's interesting is that the breach happened exactly one day after Tommy Quinn was let go."

"Wait," Cal said. "He was fired?"

"That's certainly what it looks like. There's no official two weeks notice or anything like that. I mean, I could be wrong, but see this notation here? INV? Most likely stands for 'involuntary leave'. This has all the markings of Tommy Quinn getting canned."

"Alright. Neil, you keep digging. Daniel, I think you and I

need to go back up and see the Quinns, see if they've gotten Tommy's personal things. Maybe we'll get lucky."

"What do you want us to do?" Top said.

"Why don't you and Gaucho hang tight and see what else Neil can find. We'll flex as needed."

Then, as Neil rattled off the contributors to the Washington think tank, no one thought twice when the name of Senator Warren Fowler from Wisconsin was uttered.

CHAPTER NINE

It was Cal's third trip to Roanoke in as many days. When he'd called the Quinns before leaving, just to make sure that they'd be home, Tom Quinn confirmed that they would be, and that they'd just received their son's belongings.

When they pulled up to the home, Cal was glad to see the police officer still waiting out front. He looked bored, but at least he was there.

Patty Quinn greeted Daniel and him like family.

"There's plenty of food left over from the visitation," she said. She was right, the kitchen counters were covered with food once again. "Let me fix you something."

Daniel stayed in the kitchen with Mrs. Quinn while Cal took Tom into the living room.

"I was wondering if I could take a look at your son's things and see if I might be able to find anything."

Tom stared at him and then gave a little grin. "Why do I have the feeling that you have more resources than the police?"

Cal smiled. "I'm not going to promise anything, but it can't hurt to look."

"Of course, of course. Everything's in Tommy's old room. You remember where it is."

"I do."

"Well, then I'll just be out here making sure Patty doesn't talk your friend's ear off. She's been known to take advantage of a good listener. And if I'm not mistaken, your friend Daniel there is pretty much the strong silent type."

Cal chuckled. "That he is."

"Take your time, Cal. And holler if you need me."

The bedroom was an almost cliché portrait of American youth, carefully preserved. Posters of supermodels adorned the walls. A Marines recruiting poster hung over the bed's headboard. Underneath the window overlooking the back-yard, a computer desk with a bank lamp, tidied beyond all expectation for a typical high school kid. Cal got the impression that Patty had come in here at some point after the cops left and made things up nicely.

Two rows of boxes lay along the far side of the opposite wall. Every one was marked *T. Quinn* in black Sharpie. It was obvious Patty and Tom Sr. hadn't looked through the boxes yet. They were still taped shut.

Cal thanked the gods of dumb luck when he opened the first one and found the pistol. Whoever had packed it had at least been smart enough to remove the loaded magazine and put it in a Ziploc bag, which lay neatly beside the pistol. He checked to make sure the chamber was clear, then examined the weapon in his hand. A 9mm, that's all he knew. He didn't recognize the maker.

He was about to call out to Daniel, but when he turned, the sniper was already there.

"What did you find?" Daniel asked.

"Patty chase you out already?"

"Still talking."

Cal held up the pistol. "Nine mil. I don't recognize the maker."

Daniel took the weapon and checked the clear chamber.

"I'm pretty sure it's a BUL Impact. They only made them for a few years. Pretty rare in the U.S."

"Why don't you have Neil run the serial number; he might get a hit."

Cal went back to rooting through the boxes. There were plenty of designer shirts, tailored coats, and fashionable jeans. There was a single picture, the same one he and Diane had seen on their first trip to visit the Quinns: a grinning Tommy Quinn at boot camp graduation with his parents. He set this aside and kept digging.

In the second to last box (so much for the gods of dumb luck) he found a laptop. He sat cross-legged and booted up the machine. As the home screen popped up, the computer asked for a password. Cal was no hacker, but he had something just as good. He pulled out his cellphone, tapped on the application that had been especially designed by Neil Patel himself. The app activated, and Cal set the cellphone on top of the laptop's keyboard. Immediately the app began scanning. A series of numbers and letters flashed at blinding speed across the phone screen. Then, about ten seconds later, the laptop's password screen was gone and Cal was staring at a new screen. He smiled, eternally grateful for the genius, Neil Patel.

He systematically sorted through the computer's history of activity. He analyzed the first five records that come up. The very last thing Tommy Quinn had checked on his computer was the weather. Items two and three were files he'd deleted. Like Neil always told their men, nothing was ever truly deleted, but the files were a dead end. They appeared to be old job applications and cover letters. Items four and five were routine computer processes.

It wasn't until the next batch of five items came up on the screen that Cal knew he'd hit pay dirt: emails.

The first one was addressed to his parents, just a quick hello, checking in to say he loved them. The second email, on the other hand, was addressed to someone at the Chicago Tribune with the subject line reading, "Insider Information." He scanned Tommy's email, which basically said that he had information that would impact the standing of a certain high placed lawmaker. He didn't mention which one, but he did include the words, "This politician is ground zero for what's wrong with America."

Cal sifted through five more batches of historical data, all mundane daily tasks of a man who had no idea he was about to die. He decided to give up at that point. Neil's program had already copied the entire hard drive and sent it to Neil. The Jefferson Group's big brain was no doubt already slurping up the bits of data like a digital vampire.

He texted Neil to confirm that everything was in hand, then closed the laptop and put it back in the cardboard box.

"Find anything interesting?" Tom Quinn said, entering the room.

Cal didn't want to lie to the man, but he also didn't want to get his hopes up. "That box on the bed has a pistol in it. Just wanted to make sure you knew before Patty started digging through things."

Tom walked over, lifted the cardboard lid and pulled out the weapon. The chamber was inspected for the third time that day.

"Was that Tommy's?" Cal asked carefully.

The man shook his head slowly, his face rock rigid. "I'm not sure."

"Well, if you feel uncomfortable having it in the house..."

"No, no, it's fine. I just— Why don't you take it with you? Maybe it'll help in your investigation."

"Tom, I don't know quite how to say this," Cal said awkwardly.

"I know, you're not officially investigating. I understand, but Cal, I'm not a stupid man. I know all our bills were paid this morning. There is a very short list of people in my immediate circle who might do such a thing, but none of them would have done it that way. They would have told me first. The only thing I can assume is that it was you who did it. Why, I don't know." When Cal didn't answer, he added, "That's what I thought. Thank you, son."

"My pleasure, sir."

"And as for Tommy's things, well, they're just things now, aren't they? You take whatever you need. And while it's not much, if I can be of help, I will be. All you have to do is ask."

"Thank you, Tom."

"And, Cal?"

"Yes."

"Please, find out how this happened to my boy. I know it won't bring him back, but I'll be goddamned if I have to leave this earth without at least knowing."

CHAPTER TEN

The phone call in the car with the reporter from The Chicago Tribune seemed like it wasn't going to go anywhere, especially when the guy prefaced the conversation by saying, "Look, I'm on deadline here. I can give you three minutes."

Nonetheless, Cal dove right in. "I'm calling about an email sent to you on the 23rd by one Tommy Quinn."

He knew the reporter technically didn't *have* to say anything, but to his surprise, the guy started talking, sounding fairly interested.

"Yeah, I remember. I actually talked to Tommy on the phone one time. I don't remember the conversation word for word, but I remember the vibe he gave off. He sounded... animated. Not like a lot of the kooks I get on the phone, but you could tell he was on edge. A voice like that always reminds me of those movies when somebody's being followed. Anyway, Tommy told me that he was going to deliver a flash drive with some information. I was supposed to meet him."

"Which day was that?" Cal asked.

The reporter told him.

"Well," Cal said, without missing a beat, "would it surprise you if I told you that was the day Tommy Quinn died?"

"Umm, well, yeah, that would certainly surprise me."

Cal persisted. "What happened that day?"

Now the reporter was interested, like he'd caught the scent of a juicy story. Cal could hear him scribbling in the background.

"It was the weirdest thing. I got a phone call from this think tank, don't remember the name, something based in Washington. I've got it somewhere in my notes. Here it is. The America Institute. They told me not to talk to Mr. Quinn. That's what he called Tommy, *Mr. Quinn*. The manager told me that Tommy was a disgruntled employee who got fired for poor performance. He even sent me the kid's file."

"What did it say?"

"Oh, you know, the usual stuff you'd see on any official human resources file for a terminated employee. Said he'd violated company policy, popped on one of their drug screenings. Also that he'd been stupid enough to surf porn on the company's computers."

"Do you think it was legit?"

"Who's to say? Well, anyway, the file actually had Tommy's last words that he yelled at the security guards. He said, "I'm going to bring you guys down." I thought nothing of it. Sounded like your typical kid trashing the office before he leaves, and to be quite honest with you, I've got more important things to cover than some disgruntled employee. Have you seen the murder rate in Chicago lately?"

"Yeah, I have," Cal said, "but listen, did you get anything in the mail from him or... ?"

"You're asking about the flash drive," the reporter guessed. "No, but now that you've called I'll definitely be keeping an eye out for it."

"Would you mind letting me know if you get it?"

"That depends. What's in it for me?"

Cal wasn't a fan of reporters but he decided to throw the guy a bone. "I'm conducting an independent investigation. It's personal, but I'm prepared to give you the whole story if there's anything to it."

"Deal," the reporter said. Although by now it didn't seem like he was all that interested. How often did some kook, as he'd put it, call in with some idea for a piece of ground-breaking journalism? Cal gave the man his number, thanked him, and ended the call.

"Pizza or barbecue?" Daniel said. He was at the wheel. They'd decided to go out for dinner and pick something up for the Quinns before heading back to Charlottesville.

Neil hadn't gotten any hits on the pistol, but Cal knew it was only a matter of time. Anything with a serial number had a history. Even if it was stolen, he could still track most of the owners.

"Tell me we aren't wasting our time with this," Cal said.

"We aren't wasting our time with this," Daniel said, eyes on the road ahead.

"Well, I'm glad you think so, because I'm starting to get the feeling that we're about to piss off some very important people."

Daniel chuckled. "What else is new?"

CHAPTER ELEVEN

"**W**ell, would you look at what the cat dragged in!" boomed Master Sergeant Trent when he answered the door to The Jefferson Group headquarters.

"We got stuck in traffic," Cal said. "I could use a shower and a beer, and not necessarily in that order."

"The beer I can help you with. The shower you'll have to take care of for yourself."

"Is everyone here?"

"Everyone's here. That is, everyone who's still in town."

"Tell them I'll be down in five minutes. Oh, and Top, do me a favor and don't tell me that our boy Snake Eyes looks like he just woke up from a twenty-four-hour nap."

Top chuckled and raised his hand in the air as if taking an oath, "I do solemnly swear."

THE PARED-DOWN HEADQUARTERS GROUP WAS WAITING IN the war room when Cal walked in. He felt refreshed now that he'd scraped off a few layers of road dust. He needed to call Diane at some point, but that could wait.

"Did you start without me?" Cal asked, gratefully snagging the beer offered by Top.

"Still no details on the weapon you found," Neil said, for once not clacking away on his computer. The tech genius had swapped his mouse for a chilled martini with three massive olives skewered inside.

"Any more on that think tank? What's it called again?"

"The America Institute," Daniel answered.

"Why can't I remember that?"

"Probably because it looks like one of a thousand of its kind. They do consulting, write policy paper, and do a lot of thinking, of course. They've got some big names on their register."

"And one very dead ex-employee," Cal said sipping his beer thoughtfully. "I hope you guys don't mind, but I'm going to think through this one out loud. We've got a guy who gets fired from his job. Disgruntled employee *numero uno*, aka Tommy Quinn, calls the Chicago Tribune to tell them he has some kind of evidence on a flash drive. My first question is, why not just send the files via email?"

"Maybe he thought he was being tracked," Gaucho offered.

"It's possible," Cal said, "Maybe you're right. Or maybe Tommy just liked to play spy."

"Or he could just be another disgruntled employee," Daniel added.

"True," Cal said. "But why go through all the trouble? The guy drives a hundred-thousand-dollar car, but his parents are going broke. Either he was one messed-up guy taking advantage of his parents, or he was into something deep."

"I'm sorry to tell you this, Cal," Top said. "But I'm inclined to believe option A. And to add further salt to your wound, don't forget we're not supposed to be operational right now."

Cal exhaled and took another swig of beer. It was true. After the near debacle in Europe and the way the presidential election concluded, Cal and the president agreed that maybe it was time for The Jefferson Group to lay low for a while. They deserved some time off, finally, even though that was what their trip to Europe should have been. But it seemed like every time Cal and his friends needed a breather, they got pulled back in.

"You know, Cal," Neil said, "something we haven't even discussed is whether this Quinn guy really was a criminal." Cal had thought about that, but he let Neil continue. "I mean, what if the reason he really got fired was because he was stealing information? Maybe what was on that flash drive was some top secret file from The America Institute."

"Okay, let's assume that was the case," Cal said. "Why the break-in, and why was that guy in the pickup following us the other day?"

"Maybe they were just trying to get the information back," Top said. "From what it sounds like, these guys are good. They didn't shoot back at Tom Sr., and they let you off with a warning."

Cal shifted his jaw. He could still feel the throb from that warning.

Cal looked around the room. "So are you all in agreement on this?" There were nods from Neil and Top, but Gaucho shrugged, and Daniel sat impassive as always.

"Okay, let's keep running with this. Tommy's a bad guy. He thinks stealing from The America Institute is a good idea, maybe he'll even make some money off of it, or maybe he can become some kind of a celebrity, a Julian Assange-type outlaw hero. That still doesn't explain why he died thirty yards away from where I was standing, and why, when I went to help him, he knew who I was."

"Sometimes the simplest answer is the right answer," Daniel said.

"Explain."

"Maybe it was just a coincidence that he crashed so close. And maybe he *did* know you. "

"Or maybe he'd heard about The Jefferson Group," Gaucho said.

"Where do you think he heard about us?" Cal said. "It's not like we advertise on Google or in the Yellow Pages."

"It's not impossible, Cal," Daniel said. "You know nothing's really a secret. We're consultants. Maybe someone at the America Institute or in the Corps told Tommy that we, and maybe you specifically, could be trusted. So he has a few drinks, a little liquid courage, and then he comes to find you."

"And he gets in a wreck instead? Come on, man." It felt like they were groping in the dark. "And how about this 'eyes on the prize' thing? I swear, every time I fall asleep, I hear him saying, 'Eyes on the prize. Eyes on the prize.'"

"Again," Daniel said, "maybe it's what we thought initially. He was dying and he said something that he said all the time. It was probably something he told himself every day, like a mantra, one of those pump yourself up kind of things like, 'Never stop' or, 'Just do it'."

Maybe Cal was looking into this thing with Tommy too much. It was hard to dispute what the others were saying. Maybe it *was* how it appeared: a broken guy looking for recognition. But Cal still couldn't shake the feeling that it was the wrong conclusion. There'd been something in the way that Tommy had spoken to him. So clear, so... *with purpose*.

"Alright, we'll take this slow. Neil, you keep digging on the weapon and The America Institute. The rest of us will get started on finding this flash drive, if it even exists."

"Where do you want to start?" Top asked.

Cal passed his hand over his stubbly chin, "How do you start looking for a needle in a haystack?"

"One straw at a time?"

"Exactly."

CHAPTER TWELVE

The den was dim and quiet, save for the occasional crack and fizzle from the low-burning fire. Senator Fowler inhaled the cedar scent wafting out of the massive fireplace. He and his father had built it together, with stones pulled from a nearby river and hauled a half mile to their country home in the field. His father had never shown his love outwardly, but he'd shown it in practical ways, by spending time with the young Warren, showing him how to use his hands to build, to drive a stick shift, how to rebuild an engine - all practical tools for a man of the twentieth century.

Sitting here, staring at the fire always brought back those memories. Even as a child he'd known that his father was a simple man. He himself had eclipsed his father's schooling just by finishing sixth grade. His father had not lived to see his son achieve the success he now enjoyed. And now, as he sipped his Johnnie Walker Blue Label – another outward measure of success – he wished he could go back and just be with his father one more day. Hell, he'd shovel half the horse-shit in the county if it meant just a few hours with the old man. Then, his thoughts shifted to his own son.

"Do you have children?" he asked the other man in the room.

"I do not."

"You ever want them?"

"I never really had the time, Senator."

Fowler laughed sardonically. "Time. It is a funny thing, isn't it? We fritter it away when we're children. Now I'd give away all my money, all my land, just to get a few precious moments back."

He felt free to ramble like this, knowing the other man knew better than to butt in or steer the conversation his way. It was enough for this employee to be enjoying a glass of two-hundred-and-fifty-dollar scotch with the boss.

"Let's just assume for a moment that you found out that you had a child. A son, to be exact. Now, maybe you never knew about him. Maybe he was in his twenties before you ever knew he existed. Your offspring. A gift from God. Now, assume he's a handful, that he really gives his mother hell. What do you do? Do you step in?"

"I'm not sure I understand the meaning of..."

"Just answer the question," Fowler said.

"Very well, Senator, I guess I would assess the situation. If the child was a product of... a past indiscretion, then I have to admit that I would probably deny he ever existed. Let his mother deal with it."

"You're a cold man," Fowler said, with the understanding that in any other circumstance, the man would have taken it as a compliment. He must have detected the edge in Fowler's tone because he shifted in his leather chair. It was this man's keen reading of the subtleties in Fowler's speech that made him worthy of the expensive booze.

"Senator, if I offended you, I apologize."

Fowler stared into the fire and said nothing for what felt like minutes. "I'll tell you what I would do," he said finally. "I would help that boy. I'd use all the influence I had to make sure he was well taken care of." The level of intensity in the senator's tone left no doubt that the man should remember those words. Then, Fowler's face softened. "I had a son once. Have I ever told you that?"

"No, sir, you haven't."

"Yes, well, I have. I put my heart and soul into that young man. But, as I'm sure you know, young men most often do as they please. Thank God for that, because it's the strong-willed who tend to survive. But the problem is, they don't have the benefit of decades of wisdom. I've seen your files, and by the way you carry yourself, I can tell that you've never been in a speck of trouble, have you?"

For the first time, the man looked truly uncomfortable. "No, sir."

"Don't read into the question. My point is, you'd do anything for family, and as an extension, you'd do anything for your country, wouldn't you?"

The man sat up a little straighter. "Yes, sir, I would."

"Is it just because you've sworn an oath, or do you really believe it?"

"Both, sir. I believe in this country. I fought for it."

"Well, son, I am your country now. I am your family. You belong to me, and I to you. If you go down, I go down. Is that understood?"

"Yes, Senator."

"I tell you this not to sound overly dramatic, but to make sure that you understand the gravity of the situation. You're a fine man, a war hero, but the things I'm going to ask you to do—for me, for your country—may put you at odds with the ideals of your training and the laws of the nation. Does that disturb you?"

The man licked his lips. "Senator, I've been a long-time admirer, but I've also been a lifelong student of American history. Our country needs someone like you at the helm - someone who can make the tough calls, to serve as the masthead, if you will. And, if I may be so bold as to say so, sir, I would be honored to serve you."

"Well, good," Fowler said, swirling his drink. "I'm glad we understand one another. Now, to the task at hand. I'm sure you've had ample time to digest the dossiers I gave you."

"I have."

"Here's the next step." Fowler leaned forward in his chair, as the flickering fire suddenly flared. "I want you to find this Cal Stokes, and this Marine, Daniel Briggs. They are traitors to our country. I don't just want them dead, I want them erased from history."

The young man nodded. "Yes, sir."

Fowler extended his glass in a toast. "To history."

"To history," the man repeated.

Their glasses clinked together, and Fowler savored the feeling of retribution as it wrapped around him like warm tendrils of flame from a father and son fireplace.

CHAPTER THIRTEEN

C al had just slipped under his freshly-washed sheets, his eyes already closed, when he heard a knock at the door. He groaned. After the war room meeting, Daniel had somehow convinced him to go for a run. While Cal was as fit as any elite special operator, Daniel took it to a whole other level. When they'd crested the top of O-Hill in the middle of the UVA campus, Cal thought he was going to puke. Daniel must have sensed his friend's pain, for he slowed down after that. Once Cal regained his breath, they chatted the two miles home as they ran, tossing hypotheses back and forth.

But that's all they were: hypotheses.

They were in the middle of a guessing game, an exhausting one with no end in sight. So it had been with extreme pleasure that Cal had turned off the lights in his loaned bedroom, hungry as he was for sleep. Then came the knock.

"Cal, are you awake?" It was Neil.

"I am now."

Neil didn't wait to be invited in. It was just like it was back when they had been students together at UVA. Neil had a way of ignoring other people's privacy concerns. As smart as he was, he could be clueless about social norms. As if to accentuate that point, he flipped on the light switch. Squinting, Cal shielded his eyes with his arm.

"Oh, I'm sorry. I didn't know you were in bed."

"The light was off, Neil."

"Right. Sorry. Anyway..." He took a seat on the bed without being invited. All Cal could do was laugh inside. They were like brothers after all. Cal moved over to give him room.

"So, look, I found out more information about that pistol. I was able to trace the serial number to a massive dump of outdated Israeli weaponry. The stuff was supposed to be dismantled, or whatever they do with used military stuff."

"How did it end up in the U.S.? Was it just that pistol?"

"No, that's the thing. It was a whole bunch of 'em. Hundreds."

"*Hundreds?*"

"Yeah, and they're all linked by their serial numbers. And get this, they were all headed to the same destination, a paramilitary organization called Deepwater."

"I've never heard of them," said Cal. "Wait, how'd— You mean to tell me you just found all this out in the last two hours? How? Do you have Israeli contacts I don't know about?"

Neil chuckled. "It was in the New York Times."

"*The New York Times?*"

"Yeah, get this. There was a Times story that reported the seizure of a horde of weapons and some federal arrests. They called the culprits, and I quote, 'a gang of mercenaries', like backwater militia types."

"You're not going to tell me that they've got some ranch headquarters up in Montana, are you?"

"No, it's bigger than that. They've got hideouts out west,

along the east coast, and even down in Louisiana. At least that's what The Times said. One of the guys at Deepwater was a man by the name of Kevin Branson."

"Should I know that name?"

"I don't think so. I did a quick search and found something very interesting. Branson was a former employee at The America Institute."

"Hold on. How come none of us heard about this story? You'd think that this would be big news."

Neil grinned. "It came out this past Saturday. All I can figure is, they used what the government calls its 'throw out the trash day'. Stories like that are leaked to the press on the weekend. They might include information that could be damaging to the government or maybe even one of our allies like Israel. They release it on the weekend and figure everyone's on holiday or nursing hangovers, so nobody's really paying attention. The story's out in the world, and the press and the public stays out of government's hair and off their asses."

"Please tell me you're already looking into the Institute's expenditures?"

Neil grinned like a Cheshire cat. Cal made a 'give-it-to-me' gesture.

"Remember the story about the cyber security breach at The America Institute? Well, on a whim, I cross-referenced that story with the one about the Israeli weapons coming into the U.S. Lo and behold, I found a post in an online forum called Save Our Republic. The username of the poster was TQ530."

"*TQ?* Like, Tommy Quinn?"

Neil shrugged. "It's possible. If it was him, it looks like our friend Tommy may have had more info on this and was looking for a public forum to reveal it to the world. In the post, the wording's pretty vague, but it basically accuses The

America Institute of collecting funds for purposes having nothing to do with their official charter. Are you thinking what I'm thinking?"

"That the additional information is what must be on the missing flash drive."

"That, and the fact that your uncanny ability to get us mixed up with the worst this country has to offer might be rearing its ugly head again."

"Yeah, don't remind me," Cal said, rubbing his temples.

CHAPTER FOURTEEN

Another day and another trip back to Roanoke, Virginia. Laden with coffee and bagels from Bodo's, Cal's favorite breakfast joint in Charlottesville, he and Daniel left first thing in the morning. They made good time, and Tom and Patty Quinn were waiting with more coffee when they arrived.

"Tom, I think we know why your house was burglarized," Cal said once they were inside. "We think your son might have left something here that the burglars wanted, something very important. Did Tommy have any special hiding places, like from when he was a kid? Maybe a space in the attic? Or a nook in the floorboards?"

Tom pursed his lips and shook his head slowly. "No, I don't think so. You're free to look of course."

Cal's eyes had wandered over to where Daniel was staring at the mantle over the fireplace.

"Oh my goodness," said Patty, clasping her hands before her. "You don't think he was into something awful, do you?"

"Why don't you go get some lunch ready, honey? I'm not sure you want to hear this."

"Thomas Andrew Quinn, I am not a waitress and you are not my customer. Tommy was my son, too, in case you forgot. Now, Cal, if there's something you need to tell us, please—"

"Excuse me Patty," said Daniel, "but who did the decorating on the mantle?"

Patty, momentarily flummoxed by the interruption, said, "Um, well, it was me. It's a bit dusty, as you can see." She flushed as if Daniel had pointed out an embarrassing housekeeping flaw that she'd been hiding for years.

"No ma'am. I was just noticing that everything on the mantle is so symmetrical. Statue on one side and then a statute on the other. Move on from there and you have a picture frame then matching one on the other side too."

Patty's normal color returned. "Well, yes, I do like my symmetry. Tom thinks it's a silly habit, but I like things placed where they're placed."

"Yes, ma'am," Daniel said, "but what's interesting to me is your symmetry goes on until these trophies here." He pointed to the center of the awards exhibit. "There are three of them in the middle, one on one side and two on the other."

Everyone stepped in for a closer look.

"All the rest of these were for sports, and then this one right here was for chess club." Daniel pointed to one of the trophies, the smallest of the bunch, a gold statue of a king chess piece. "*Eighth grade*," Daniel read aloud, squinting at the small plaque. "Why would he display an eighth grade chess club trophy next to his college track awards?"

The Quinns looked at each other. "I don't know," Patty said. "I hadn't really noticed. Things had been difficult for him. Maybe he just put it there one day."

Tom Quinn nodded. "He had a place of his own, but he liked to store most of his older stuff here in our house. Maybe he just forgot to put that one away."

Cal stepped over and lifted up the trophy. It rattled just

perceptibly as soon as it left the mantle.

There's something inside, he thought. He turned it over and looked at the green felt on the bottom. There was no sign of it being tampered with, but when he grabbed one of the corners and peeled it back, it came off easily. He flipped the trophy over and dumped a shiny metal key into his palm.

The Quinns stared at the key, wide-eyed.

Daniel took the offered key from Cal and inspected it. "Patty, did your son have a cell phone on him when he died?"

"Why, yes," she said haltingly.

"I think it's in our room," Tom said.

"Would you like me to fetch it for you?"

"Please," Cal said.

When she left the room, Tom said, "I really didn't want her to know any more of this."

"We understand," Cal said.

"It's been hard for her. I'd like to spare her any more pain—"

He cut himself short as Patty returned moments later, cradling the phone like it was a prized possession. She held it up for Cal and Daniel to see.

"Do you mind if we borrow this?" Cal said. "I promise we'll bring it back."

"Of course," she said. She handed the phone to him slowly, staring at it, as if reluctant to allow any more of Tommy Quinn be taken from her.

Cal pressed the home button, and the phone came to life and prompted him for a password, a ten-digit password no less.

He held the screen up for Daniel to see. Daniel squinted at it, then returned his gaze. Cal knew exactly what the look meant.

Someone out there was making it damn hard for them to get any information on this case.

CHAPTER FIFTEEN

The man in the navy blue ski jacket stepped out of a Hyundai rental car and surveyed the library parking lot. Minimal traffic. Perfect. He hadn't been to a library in years. There had been that time in his junior year of high school with Caroline—

He stopped himself there. His mind was wandering again. Unprofessional.

The man refocused on the library and walked inside, passing an elderly couple shuffling out arm in arm. The interior of the library was as quiet as a funeral home and smelled like old paper and wet people. There were two levels, and while the place wasn't stately in the way a metropolitan downtown library was, the floors shined, and not a thing looked out of place. The librarian at the checkout counter didn't look up as he passed. No one did, as if there was some unspoken rule that when you were in a library, you weren't supposed to make eye contact.

It was perfect for what he was doing.

Once he made it to the second floor, he took out his cell phone and checked the text message one more time. *306.7*

VAT, page 43. The man scanned the rows. It took him less than a minute to find the area he needed. The numbers in the text took him to a neglected corner, a place even quieter than the rest of the library. *A place Caroline would have liked*, he thought, but then pushed the memory away. *Focus.*

All sounds became muted, as if he was in a dead room layered with studio-grade insulation. He looked down the opposite aisle and saw another patron sitting by the second story railing, reading what looked like a coin-collecting magazine. The old man had a perfect view of him but didn't seem to care. Nothing felt out of place.

The newest visitor to the library turned to the stacks and ran his fingers along the spine of each book. *304, 305, 306,* and then there it was 306.7 VAT. There was no title on the spine, but then he pulled it out and saw the title of the book: *Kama Sutra, The Art of Love*. His face scrunched with confusion. He checked the spine again, *306.7 VAT*. It was the correct book, alright. Was this some kind of joke? *No*, the man told himself. *This is the spy business.*

He thumbed to page 43. Before his eyes, a picture of a naked couple tangled in a knot. It reminded him of something he'd seen in a Cirque du Soleil commercial, where two acrobats had wriggled together, looking more like writhing snakes than humans.

The man shook his head, and then he noticed it. A thin piece of paper inserted in the crease of the spine. He took one more look around. No cameras. No eyes. The man with the coin-collecting magazine definitely couldn't see him or what he was doing.

He pulled out the piece of paper. On it was written a single address: 246 Flynn Street, Unit 161B. The man closed his eyes and repeated the address three times. Then he opened them and read the note again. It was good that his once-sharp memory was back. The therapy had helped after all.

Thanks to the senator, he was back on his own feet. It felt good to be doing something again. And something for his country, no less. Something for a man who, he was almost embarrassed to admit, made him feel a little star struck. Senator Warren Fowler was a great man, a patriot, a public servant whose only focus in life was service to his country.

The man in the navy ski jacket smiled, and then opened his mouth and popped in the note he'd just crumpled in his hand. He chewed it a few times, feeling it soften and begin to dissolve, then swallowed. The evidence was gone.

His target now acquired, the Kama Sutra was reinserted into its library home. The spy looked around again and could have sworn the old man with the magazine had waggled the periodical his way, as if waving hello, but there was no eye contact. The weary patron was fully engaged in his reading, or at least that's what the younger man thought.

His confidence renewed, the man in the blue coat left the way he'd come. He took his time to get a sip from the water fountain, just to make sure he wasn't being followed. Then not five minutes after he'd arrived, he left in the same Hyundai sedan. His spirit invigorated. His vision clear. The veteran soldier-turned-spy felt whole for the first time in months.

CHAPTER SIXTEEN

Cracking Tommy Quinn's code was apparently as easy as plugging a charging cable from his phone into Cal's, which had been preloaded with Neil's magic software. After beaming info from Tommy's phone to Neil's laptop, Cal and Daniel pulled into a Walmart parking lot and waited for Neil's Facetime call to come in. Not more than two minutes passed before it did.

"Okay," Neil said, "so the phone looks clean. No spooky bogey-man virus that jumped out and attacked my system. Now, that's not to say Tommy didn't have some safeguards. He had your everyday, run-of-the-mill security stuff on there. Then two higher-grade, maybe military- or intelligence service-type programs that took a minute to break through. It's actually quite a simple process when you have the right equipment. You start with a..."

Neil went on to explain the intricacy of breaking into a phone without alerting anyone monitoring the device that it was being tampered with. Then again, he may have been explaining the inner-workings of a nuclear accelerator. It didn't matter by that point. It sounded like Greek to the Marines in the car.

Cal looked at Daniel. His stoic friend had an amused grin on his face.

"Where will you start?" Daniel asked, drawing Neil's attention back to the task at hand.

He turned his camera and mounted it so the men could see Neil's computer screen. And the cell phone beside it. "What's on my screen is exactly what's on Tommy's phone. Hope it's clear enough for you to see."

"We see it. Go on."

Neil made his way through Tommy's phone. A few clicks and a scroll, and a series of letters and numbers appeared on the laptop screen.

"Okay," Neil said, "you see these gray areas here? That's all deleted stuff. Pictures, texts, whatever. But the good news is, whatever info it is, it has its own code series. All we have to do to find the deleted text is to isolate the code series. The prefix is repeated here, here, here, and so on. They're all relatively small files, so they have to be texts." The call went silent as Neil diligently went back to work. Another few clicks and the scroll code reduced. "Okay, that's better. I just sorted them by date. You think we should start on the day Tommy died, or maybe a couple of days before?"

"Let's go with a day or two before to start."

More clicking and scrolling, then Neil cut and pasted a huge chunk of the data into an entirely new order.

"Status report, Neil," Cal said, throwing an eye roll toward Daniel.

"Well if you really want to know, basically my computer is running a limited random number analysis based on an algorithm of my own creation that analyzes data sets within select symmetric encryption modules."

Cal put his head in his hand, rubbed vigorously, then lifted his head and said, "Sounds terrific."

A couple more minutes of silence, then, "Okay, I've got it ... just about there... annnnd... there we go."

The text on the laptop had changed from gibberish to actually legible.

"That's more like it," Cal murmured.

Neil was scrolling slowly now so they could all read. Then, there it was. Plain as day.

Cal pointed. "*Eyes on the prize*," he said. The message had been sent to a 703 area code. The reply from the same number was an address: 246 Flynn Street, Unit 161B. "What is that, an apartment?"

"Give me a second," Neil said. "No. Storage facility. And I just ran the number. It's unlisted, probably a burner phone."

Everyone fell silent, digesting the most recent revelation. Was the storage unit where Tommy hid the flash drive? And whom had he texted? Another reporter like the guy from the Chicago Tribune?

"I've got an idea," Cal said after staring at the address for a few moments. "Neil, can I send a text from Tommy's phone without being traced to our current location?"

Cal could almost hear the roll of Neil's eyes. "Have you forgotten who you're talking to? If I wanted to, I could probably run an entire drug empire with your phone alone. Hold on, give me a second. Okay, there. It's set."

Cal picked up Tommy's phone and sent the following text: "246 Flynn Street, 161B. Key in my possession. I'll bring the cash. Meet in one hour."

"Okay, we're all set," Cal said.

A moment later, and Neil had the information in front of him. "Whoa," he said. "Are you sure that was smart? You don't even know who that went to."

"We don't have time to be messing around with this anymore," Cal said. "Better to flush them out and see what happens. I'm done waiting. My GPS says this address is thirty minutes away. I say we get there early and see what we can find."

CHAPTER SEVENTEEN

The storage facility at 246 Flynn Street was one of those modern monstrosities with its name, Storenow.com, splashed across the side in green and white. It stuck out in the quiet suburb like an elephant in a swimming pool. Three stories, maybe four if there was a level below ground. It was all indoor and fully climate controlled. By sheer luck, there was no keypad access or any kind of gatekeeper manning the entrance.

There were two parking lots on either side of the building. Each had their own entrance. Cal couldn't decide whether it was a good or a bad thing that there were camera domes all along the perimeter. Good, because if there was going to be trouble, maybe the cameras would deter it. Bad, because if there was going to be trouble, Cal and Daniel would be in full view. As if to accentuate the point they were greeted by a domed camera as soon as they walked inside.

"Might as well just smile and wave," Cal said under his breath.

They found their way to the second level, opting for a concrete stairway over the freight elevator that, given their luck, would malfunction at some critical moment. The second story of 246 Flynn Street was a long hallway of storage units. There was a right turn up ahead. Unit 161B was up around that bend. In fact, it was right at the turn.

Cal spotted the number 161B over the shoulder of a hard-faced kid holding a very familiar weapon, a replica of the BUL Impact he'd found amongst Tommy Quinn's things.

"Hands up," the young man said.

Cal noticed the high and tight haircut, and the steel in the young man's eyes. He was rail thin, but the steady weapon in his hand left no doubt as to his intent.

"I think there's been some misunderstanding," Cal said. "And besides, there's cameras all over this place." Refusing to raise his hands, Cal motioned with his chin to a dome just over his head.

"I'm tight with the guy that owns this place. He turned the cameras off for me."

"You could have smiled after all," Daniel mumbled.

Cal ignored him. "And why would your friend do a thing like that?"

"He's a friend."

"Oh, I get it, he turns off the camera because he picks out the storage unit he wants you to break into and which customers he wants you to hold up."

"No, it's not like that. We served together and—" The kid stopped, realizing he'd said too much. "Enough talking. Let me see those hands raised."

Cal nodded to Daniel. They both did as instructed.

"I want to see that key."

"What key?" Cal replied.

"Don't play stupid. You texted me."

"Kid, I have no idea what you're talking about."

"I know it was you. I've seen you before."

"Excuse me," came a deep voice from behind the boy.

The Israeli weapon-toting kid didn't shift his weapon from Cal and Daniel, but he did shift his feet and turn his head just slightly so he could see the imposing figure of Willie Trent smiling down at him.

"Do you happen to know where I can get a good back rub in this town?"

The comment made the kid turn one half a degree too much, and Cal made his move, jumping the kid and placing him in a headlock as Daniel relieved the young man of his firearm. To his credit, the kid thrashed vigorously and almost got away, but Cal applied just enough pressure on the boy's carotid arteries, his arm forming a perfect 'V' under the stranger's chin. The kid actually tapped Cal's arm twice, the universal signal of 'I give.'

"Who are you?" Cal rasped in the boy's ear.

The kid straightened up just a bit. "Sir, Corporal Bryan Edgerton, United States Marine Corps."

"Well, then," Top said. "Corporal, you are in the presence of a Marine Master Sergeant, the illustrious Willie Trent." He gave a slight bow. "The man over there with your weapon is Staff Sergeant Daniel "Snake Eyes" Briggs. Trust me when I tell you, you don't want to mess with him. And the man holding you, well, I forget what rank he was, but he was a pretty good Marine too, I think."

Cal could feel the muscles in the corporal's body go slack.

"Sir, is the Master Sergeant going to take me to the cops, sir?"

"First of all, call me Willie, or Top. I'm no longer on the active duty rolls of the Marine Corps. Second, whether we take you to the cops depends on what you say in the next five minutes. Do you understand me, Corporal?"

"Yes, Master—, yes, Top."

"Very well. Cal, I believe this young man has a story to tell us. Would you be so kind as to let our new friend fill his lungs with air for just a moment?"

It took every ounce of control Cal had not to chuckle. Top just had that effect, even if you'd just been held up at gunpoint.

"There, that's better now," Top said. "Corporal, you have me entranced. Do tell us what your affiliation is, or was, with Tommy Quinn?"

It took a couple beats for Corporal Edgerton to gather his thoughts, but once he had, he clasped his hands behind his back in a modified parade rest.

"Lance Corporal Quinn was one of my Marines," Edgerton explained.

"One of *your* Marines?" Top asked, shooting a glance at Cal. "You're just out of diapers, son. Tommy Quinn had to have had a good ten, fifteen years on you."

"Yes, Top. We were in the reserves together. He got out a while back, but you know how it is. He'll always be one of my Marines."

Top nodded his understanding. "Ah. Continue."

"Tommy was a good kid," Edgerton said, the irony of the statement not lost on any of the three of the Marines standing before him. "Good shot. One of the best PTers we had. But he missed a couple drills and then got busted down for missing an overseas movement. I stood up for him, but the colonel didn't much care. Tommy knew the writing was on the wall, so he got out. I tried to keep tabs on him, and he'd stop by every once in a while to bring me a fancy six-pack of beer or some bottle of liquor I couldn't pronounce. We did one tour overseas together, you know. I was brand new at the time and, well, he showed me the way, taught me that a 130-pound soaking wet Marine could just as easily lead a man like yourself, Master Sergeant, as anyone could. He just had to prove himself."

"You've got that right, Corporal," Top said. "One of the best Marines I ever had the privilege of serving under was a 115-pound corporal who happened to be a high school drop-out."

Corporal Edgerton nodded and went on. "I've been pretty busy the last year trying to go active-duty, but I'd text Tommy every once in a while just to see how he was doing. He said he was busy too, but then the last couple months he just, I don't know, he started acting weird. On one of the last calls, he was babbling, I couldn't understand half the words he said. Then the very last time I talked to him, he said he had some flash drive that he wanted to deliver to someone up in Chicago."

"The Chicago Tribune?" said Cal.

"Yeah, that's it. The Chicago Tribune. He didn't tell me what was on it, and I didn't ask. The last thing he texted me was the address of this storage unit. You think it's weird that I know the owner? You think maybe Tommy knew that?" He didn't wait for an answer. "Well, anyway, I got a note in the mail the next day. I knew it was Tommy's handwriting because his handwriting was terrible, but even still this was pretty bad. I had to read it three times just to understand what he was telling me to do. He said he wanted me to break into his parents' house because they, quote, 'couldn't be dragged into this', unquote. Didn't say what *this* was. He said he was going away for a while. He said I would be compensated after it was delivered to the reporter at the Tribune, and that it would help take down some bad people. I didn't do it for money. I did it for him. I didn't want to see his parents get hurt. They're good people."

"You've met the Quinns?" Cal said.

"A few times. His mom would even call me just to check on Tommy, even though she knew he wasn't serving with me anymore. You can probably figure out the rest of the story." He cast furtive glances at the men, mouth moving as if he was nervous about what to say next. "I've... seen you guys at the Quinn's house. I'm the one who broke in."

"You're awfully lucky Mr. Quinn's bullet missed you. What did Tommy ask you to retrieve?"

"He said there was a chess trophy on the mantle with a key inside for the storage unit. I must have made too much noise because Mr. Quinn came out before I could get to it. There was no chance to go back in, what with the cops hanging out there."

"You've been watching us?" Cal asked.

Corporal Edgerton nodded. "I've been right across the street. That house is for sale, and my sister is a realtor. I knew how to get in."

Top shook his head with an ear to ear grin. "Well, you are full of surprises, aren't you, Corporal?"

"I hope this won't get the Quinns in any trouble," Edgerton said quickly. "I've been trying to figure out a way to help them since Tommy died. Talked to the VA and tried to see if maybe they could get some kind of compensation, what with Tommy going crazy. I just feel like I could have helped him."

"Did he give you that gun?" Cal asked, pointing to the weapon in Daniel's hand.

"Yes, sir, he did. It was a present for my birthday."

"I'll make sure it gets back to you," Cal said. "But we need to have it checked out first, if that's okay."

"Yes, sir, that's fine. I've got my own weapons at home. Like I said, I didn't mean any trouble. I thought I was doing the right thing."

"But you knew Tommy was dead."

"Yes, sir, I did."

"And what about the text we sent you? Why did you come?"

Edgerton wet his lips. "Have you ever been in one of

those situations where you just know it's the right thing to do, no matter the danger? Well, this was one of those times. I know you guys could have been the bad guys, but I had to confront you. I had to get answers."

"You were still helping Tommy," Daniel said.

"Yes, sir. I guess I was." Then his face brightened. "I took some time off from my day job. If you guys would like my help, I'm happy to do it."

Cal wasn't sure he wanted to bring the young corporal into their mess, but he said, "Why don't you head out with Top. He can give you a ride home if you need. And Top, get Corporal Edgerton's information. I think he's proven that he's more than capable."

"You got it," Top said and then draped an arm over Corporal Edgerton's shoulder, ushering him towards the far end of the hallway. "Corporal, I think you and I are going to be great friends. Now, let me tell you about the time your new friend, Willie Trent, saved the life of a young pup named Calvin Stokes Jr." He smiled back at Cal, who broke into a silent laugh.

The conversation disappeared down the hall, leaving Cal and Daniel in front of unit 161B. "Well, that was an interesting twist," Cal said. "You don't seem surprised."

Daniel shrugged. "Things have a way of working out."

"Okay, Zen master. Why don't we give this a try." Cal took the key from his pocket and opened the storage unit. Inside the roughly five-by-ten stall was an old wooden chair, and on top of it, a mahogany cigar box. Cal opened it slowly. Inside was a note that simply said, "I'm sorry for everything. Please, take care of my family." Underneath the note was the picture they'd seen many times before, the one of Tommy at boot camp graduation, flanked by his smiling parents.

Underneath the picture was a black flash drive.

"Bingo," Cal said. He pocketed the flash drive, closed the

cigar box, and put it under his arm. "Come on, let's get out of here before Edgerton's friend turns the cameras back on."

They were back on the street in minutes, heading towards the car.

"Have you told Diane what's going on yet?" Daniel asked.

"I don't really have the time." Cal sighed. He knew it was a lame answer.

"I don't think you should wait on that. Remember what you promised her."

"I know, I know."

Just then, as they were not ten feet from the car, a Hyundai sedan zoomed into the parking lot. Cal glanced towards the vehicle, saw the masked face of the driver, and then the barrel of a weapon.

He bolted just as the rattle of automatic gunfire exploded in the suburban parking lot, sending a spray of bullets straight for Daniel and him.

CHAPTER EIGHTEEN

He was just quick enough, diving behind a parked vehicle, as bullets scorched the air where he'd been standing not a millisecond before. Daniel found cover behind a much sturdier dumpster.

"Friend of yours?" Daniel asked from across the way.

"I don't think he's on my Christmas list." Cal answered.

Cal couldn't shake the feeling that whoever the masked man was, he was an amateur, with the melodramatic screeching of tires as he came into the parking lot. An un-silenced weapon in public was one thing, maybe the sound was supposed to deter civilians from stepping in, but Cal knew it was only a matter of time before the police showed up. He and Daniel were both armed, of course, and there would probably be a few hard questions should they defend themselves on America's streets, but Cal already had enough complications in his life. Time to get creative.

When he looked up at the vehicle he was hiding behind, he was surprised to see that it wasn't a car at all. It was a delivery van. But not just any delivery van. It was one of those vending machine companies. He knew he was taking a chance, but he reached up and grabbed the latch, praying that it was unlocked. Luck was with him, because the door slid open and inside he found a woman in her fifties, crouched, hands over her head.

Her eyes snapped open when Cal opened the door. He put a finger to his lips and looked around. Ho-Ho's. Potato chips. Wide mouth bottles of soda. And then he had it. He grabbed two items and slipped back out of the van, more bullets shredding the thin metal overhead.

He got to a place where Daniel could see him and held up the two items. Daniel smiled. The firing abated, but when Daniel peeked out from around the dumpster, his move was answered by more rounds fired. Now Cal could sense more than see something else was happening. The man in the Hyundai was moving to a more advantageous position. Maybe he wasn't an amateur after all.

We'll have to see about that, Cal thought. He twisted open the plastic Coca-Cola bottle, and then tore open the package of Mentos. He popped two into his hand and one in his mouth. The two in his hand went into the Coke bottle, fizzing upon contact. He followed up with a few more and quickly screwed the cap back on. Once he had it secure he shook it a few times and then looked back at Daniel.

Cal had no idea where the enemy vehicle was, but he was pretty sure that Daniel had a clear view, given that he was closer. The chemical combination in his hand was almost ready. He locked eyes with Daniel, who nodded. They'd only get one shot at this, and man, it would be a stupid way to die. Cal had faith in his friend. When had ol' Snake Eyes missed before?

Tamping down his last inkling of doubt, Cal tossed the bottle underhanded to Daniel, and with the same move, he turned to the open van, grabbed two more bottles one in each hand. He gave two slow nods Daniel's way as if counting down, "3, 2, ..." and then he exploded from behind the van chucking the ineffectual bottles of soda towards the Hyundai. He immediately received a furious rattle of gunfire in response.

Good, Cal thought, as he ducked back under cover, nearly falling over in his haste to get out of the line of fire. But he smiled grimly as the bullets tore through metal and he saw that Daniel was no longer behind the dumpster. Cal didn't have to risk another peek towards their attacker. He heard the tell-tale BOOM moments later, and a scream. It wasn't Daniel's scream, it was the gunman who'd just gotten a face full of exploding plastic, Coca-Cola, and Mentos.

Cal rushed out from behind the van just in time to see Daniel dragging the man from the vehicle and slamming him face down on the ground. Now came the siren wails.

"Should we wait?" Daniel asked, planting a foot on the back of the man's neck to stop him from writhing.

It only took Cal a split second to make the decision. "Put him in our car. Let's get out of here."

Daniel dragged the perpetrator back to their vehicle as Cal did a quick search of the Hyundai. It was clean except for the automatic H&K in the passenger seat lying in a nest of shells and empty magazines. Cal left the weapon just in case they were stopped, and then ran to where Daniel was waiting with their prisoner already tied up in the back.

"Let's go." Cal pulled out his phone and dialed Neil.

"*Geek Squad, how may I help you?*"

"No time for fun and games, Neil. We've got a complication."

"*What's up?*"

"Remember that storage facility? We're gonna need you to make sure there's no video footage of us there."

"*No problem*," Neil answered. "*Anything else?*"

Cal thought about it for a moment. It never failed to

amaze him how quickly Neil could respond to seemingly impossible tasks. "No, I think we're good for now."

"*Hey, Cal?*"

"Yeah?"

"*Diane stopped by a few minutes ago. She said—*"

"Damn it, we were supposed to meet for lunch."

"*Yeah, that's what she said. She used worse words though.*"

"Did you tell her where I was?"

"*Um, no, I said I didn't know. I figured it was probably better coming from you.*"

"Yeah, thanks."

Daniel was easing out of the parking lot now. No need to rush, no need to make a scene. They hadn't gotten a block down the street when three police cruisers zoomed by, not one policeman giving them a second glance.

"Is she still there?" Cal said.

"*No, she left. She said she'd call you.*"

Cal felt his phone buzz in his hand. He looked down on the screen and there she was.

"Neil, I've got to go."

"*Alright, but tell me if—*"

Cal switched the phone call over, ready for his second battle of the day. "Hey babe, we were just talking about you."

"*Yeah, we were supposed to meet for lunch.*"

Cal tried to gauge whether she was truly upset from the handful of words. It was a useless task.

"Honey, I'm so sorry about that. I'll make it up to you, I promise."

"*Cal, do I hear sirens?*"

"What? Oh yeah, I, uh..." The lie almost came out too easily.

"*Cal, what's going on?*"

"I'm fine, it's okay, I just..." Cal exhaled. "There's a lot I need to tell you when I get back. Will you be around?"

"*Sure, I don't have to leave until tomorrow morning. Cal, are you...*"

"Like I said, I'm fine, but, well, this thing with the Quinns kind of took a turn."

Now Diane's voice was hard. "*Don't tell me now. You tell me when you get home.*"

Cal was about to answer, when he realized the call was over.

"I told you. You should have called her," Daniel said.

"Yeah, yeah. Let's just get out of here before the lady in the delivery van tells the police what happened."

CHAPTER NINETEEN

It was decided that going all the way back to Charlottesville with their prisoner would be too risky. Top suggested on the phone that they find a place to hole up and talk to their new acquaintance.

"*I know a place about thirty minutes from here,*" he said. "*Let me find the address and I'll text it to you. We'll go in and make the preparations.*"

"What did you do with our pal from the storage unit?"

"*Edgerton? I dropped him off at home. He's a good kid, Cal. I think we should leave him out of this.*"

"I agree. Okay. Let me know when you're ready, and we'll meet you there."

The formerly masked man was now doing his best to play the role of stoic prisoner. He hadn't said a word in response to any of Cal's questioning.

"That was a friend of mine," Cal said to the captive. "His arms are about as thick as my thigh. He sure does enjoy making people talk. I suggest you start talking before we go meet him. I'd hate to see what might happen later." The man still remained silent. "You know, it doesn't look like whoever sent you is coming to help. Oh, and didn't anyone tell you that *we* are the good guys?"

"Traitor," the man blurted.

It wasn't the response that Cal had expected. Maybe a "fuck you" or "I'm going to kill you when I get my hands on you," but *traitor?*

Forty-five minutes later, they pulled into the gravel parking lot of a ramshackle motel, the VACANCY light on the decrepit sign flickering its Y overhead. The lights in the motel office were low. Cal could see that there was a TV on. Whoever was manning the desk wasn't concerned enough to come to the window when they pulled into the lot.

Cal wanted to ask Daniel if he really thought this was a good idea. Something more private would have worked better. But Cal had to trust his friends. It wasn't until he opened the car door that he thought he might have an idea of what Top and Gaucho were up to. Music thumped from the Marine master sergeant's oversized Ford F350 at the end of the row, even though there was no one inside the cab.

Cal kept a hand on his weapon as Daniel undid the binds that tied the man's hands to his feet. Their prisoner remained still and calm.

"You make one wrong move and I'll put you down," Cal said.

A flicker of fear in the man's eyes. At least he wasn't a complete nut.

Cal counted fifteen motel rooms. To his surprise, or maybe naïve shock, there were blaring televisions and radios emitting their cacophony from nearly every rented room. When they finally approached the room that Top had reserved for them, the music was even more deafening. Cal didn't have to knock. The door was propped open with the deadbolt. The three men stepped inside.

"Welcome to the party," Top said. He had his shirt

stripped off, flaunting his chiseled form, and he held two beers in the air. Their prisoner's wide eyes took in every detail of the room, especially the hulking Master Sergeant Trent, who walked over and placed a massive hand on the back of the man's neck.

"My friends tell me you like to party," Top said, and then pointed to the other man in the room. Gaucho was sitting in the corner, a beer in one hand, a silenced pistol in his lap. "You make one wrong move, and my buddy over there will make sure this is your last hoorah." Then the massive Marine turned his attention back to the newcomers. "Cal, why don't you grab yourself a beer. Daniel, the water's in the cooler. I'm going to make our new friend comfortable."

There was no cooler, but Top and Gaucho had apparently stopped at the store on the way in. The bathtub was full of ice. Nestled within were an open case of beer and a 12-pack of water, untouched, and some sandwiches. This definitely wasn't supposed to be a party, Cal thought, yet his friends had seen fit to prepare them for a long night. What Cal really wanted to do was ask how Top knew to come to a place with such advantageous obscurity, and in the middle of the day no less. But when he emerged from the bathroom, two bottles of water in hand, he saw that Top was busy cinching down the last rope across their visitor's legs.

"There we go," Top declared. "Snug as a bug."

He motioned the others over, and there was a quick huddle of the four Jefferson Group men, during which time it was determined that Top would take the lead on the interrogation. Not one of them wanted to resort to torture, but if it came to that, well, so be it.

Next, they all gathered around the man tied to the chair. He'd been stripped of his navy blue ski jacket. The music from the speakers Top had brought was still blaring, some awful Top 40 bubble gum crap, but no such cacophony was any match for Top's booming baritone.

"Judging by the fact that we did not find a wallet on your person, I figure it might not be your intent to reveal your name. But let me tell you this, my friend, one way or another, we will get what we need. So, why don't you save us the trouble and start by telling us who you are."

The man was looking up at him now with obvious hatred in his eyes. There was fear there too. It was impossible not to be afraid, unless you were crazy. And this man was not crazy.

"They're going to find you, you know," he said.

Top smiled. "Who is going to find us?"

"You'll see soon enough," the man said, and then spat on the floor.

"Do you like kids, my friend?"

The man didn't answer.

"I can tell you like kids. You don't seem like a bad guy. You might even like to have kids one day." Top moved closer and placed a hand on the man's shoulder. "Now I'm not sure who trained you, but I can bet that you know it doesn't take much for a man to break." Top's leg bent and his knee rested right at the pressure point between the man's legs. "You see, I am not a bad man and I do not like to see other men in pain, but you shot at my friends. And I am willing to use every trick at my disposal to ensure I find out who you are, who you work for, and what you've been up to." Top leaned forward and applied just enough pressure to see the man's eyes bulge.

"Lester Howe," the man blurted.

Top eased off with his knee. "Is that your name?"

The man bobbed his head quickly, taking in gasps of air.

"Well, Lester, thank you for that. See how easy that was? Now, Lester, whom do you work for?"

"The United States Army."

The four Jefferson Group warriors exchanged looks.

"Why do I have a feeling you're lying to me, Lester?" Top leaned in with his knee again.

Lester squirmed. "No, I swear, I swear. I'm in the Army!"

Top eased off. "Are you telling me that the United States Army sent you after us? Do you even know who we are?"

Lester looked confused now, his eyes darting to the door as if his rescuers might come in at any second.

Another lean in the crotch. "I asked you a question, Lester."

"Okay, okay. I'm not in the Army. I mean, I was, but I got out."

"Why?"

Lester looked like he might try to resist, but one look down at Top's knee made him reconsider. "I had problems, okay?"

"What kind of problems?"

"I didn't know how to cope. I came back and got in some trouble. My dad helped me."

"Is it your dad that's behind this?

"No, no. He has nothing to do with it. He just introduced me to..."

"Introduced you to *whom*, Lester?" Top asked, tipping the chair back onto its back legs.

"Someone in the U.S. government. Someone who..."

"Someone who what?"

"Someone who knows all about you."

"*Moi?*" Top asked, pointing at himself.

"No, them. Stokes and Briggs."

Another hard lean in. The man's face contorted in agony.

"Would you like to tell me why *your* oh-so-important friend doesn't like *my* friends?"

"He said they committed treason, that they spied on our government and shared the information with foreign power.

He said they're traitors." Lester regained composure now and he glared at Cal and Daniel.

Cal couldn't help but compare himself to the man. He would have felt the same way had the roles been reversed. The man was obviously telling the truth, at least the truth that he had been led to believe.

"He's a great man, you know," Lester said. "He's going to return this country to what it should be. If I have anything to say about it, he's going to be president one day."

Top leaned in again, applying even more pressure this time. "I don't seem to remember telling you that you had any kind of say in this room."

Lester let out a moan of pain and then Top stepped back. Lester huffed to get his breath back. To everyone's surprise, he started speaking again. "I pledge allegiance to the flag of the United States of America and to the Republic for which it stands..."

"I don't believe what I'm hearing." Top whispered in Cal's ear. "Is this boy crazy? I think he really believes in what he's doing."

Lester finished the pledge.

Top asked, "Who sent you, Lester?"

There was something else in Lester's eyes now: Not the maniacal gleam of a psychopath, or the numb look of a man broken on the rack. This was the pride of a man who's resigned to his fate, fought off his attackers for hours, and was finally out of ammunition.

"It doesn't really matter if I tell you, you know. He's untouchable."

Cal was about to tell the man sitting before him that no one was untouchable, but the comment was unnecessary.

Lester went on. "He told me all about you two. You pretend to do the right thing. You say what you're doing is for the good of America. He sees right through you. You're traitors, and it is my wish that he drags you before the American people and exposes you for the frauds you are."

"Who is *he*?" Cal snapped.

Lester smiled up at him. "Senator Warren Fowler."

"Hold on," Cal said, "why do I know that name?" Then it came to him. "The Chairman of the Republican National Committee, the guy from Wisconsin?"

Lester nodded.

"What does he want with us?"

"I told you," Lester said. "He's going to find you, and he's going to kill you."

CHAPTER TWENTY

Cal was so lost in thought when he entered the home he and Diane shared that it took him a moment to realize she was sitting right there in the dimly-lit living room. A half-finished bottle of Chardonnay sat on the coffee table, and Diane cradled what looked like the other half in her hand.

"You never called," Diane said. It wasn't an observation – rather, an accusation delivered with the deadly accuracy of a spear thrust.

"Yeah," Cal exhaled, ready to take the heat. He knew he had screwed up, but he couldn't remember ever seeing Diane like this. "Things got a little out of hand today and I... just kind of forgot."

"You seem to be forgetting a lot of things these days," Diane said, raising her glass for a sip.

Silently, he dumped his things onto an armchair and went to sit next to her on the sofa. She inched over, offering her cheek instead of a kiss on the lips.

"Do you mind if I grab a glass?" he asked motioning to the bottle of wine.

"This is your world. Do whatever you want."

"Okay. Maybe I won't grab a glass then. Do you want to tell me what's got you all riled up?"

Diane turned slowly. "If you have to ask me that, Cal Stokes, you're either the stupidest man I've ever met or you're trying to get under my skin."

"I'd rather get you under the sheets, but—"

"Don't even start," she said, putting up a hand. Her tone could have disarmed a terrorist.

"Alright, I'm sorry." There was no use explaining to her how there had been no time to think on the ride back from the crappy motel. Added to the mental jumble were the discussion at The Jefferson Group headquarters and then the final revelation from Lester Howe. Cal's mind was doing loops. "Look, I said I was sorry, okay? What else do you want me to do?"

"I want you to tell me what's going on."

"Babe, look... you're just starting a new job. Maybe it's better if—"

"Do not give me the national security line. I've been privy to plenty of information in the past few months. The president trusts me. Why don't *you* trust me?"

"It's not that I don't trust you, I just... you're right. I should have told you. But it's not my fault."

"That sounds lame, even from you." She then took a long drink of chardonnay, wiped the corner of her lip with her thumb, and said, "I seem to remember a certain Marine making me a promise a couple months ago. Let's see if you remember. We were on vacation in Paris, having a great time, and then all hell breaks loose and Brandon kills that lunatic, Tony McKnight. We all agreed, including the president, that it was time to lay low. He can't take the heat. You can't risk the exposure. And above all, we are trying to build a life together. Am I remembering that correctly?"

"Yes, but—"

"There is no *but*, Cal. By the way, I'm not an idiot. I saw how you walked in here all lost in thought. I can tell you are not going to let this thing go. So where does that leave me? Where does it leave *us?*"

"Look, you knew who you were dating before—"

Diane put up her hand again. "Don't even give me that line about me not supporting you. You're pissing down the wrong hole with that one, Marine."

Pissing down the wrong hole, Marine? Cal thought. *Sheesh*. She was really mad.

Diane went on. "I serve this country too, you know. I believe in it. I think we should find the bad guys and take them out. You've always known that about me, but what you're doing, Cal, it's reckless. I go to work every day thinking that this is the day you'll be caught, that all your tricks of the trade won't get you out of being handcuffed by some two-bit cop who goes by the books. Or maybe Daniel won't be there to save you. Or Top or Gaucho won't swoop in at the last minute like the friggin' cavalry."

"I can take care of myself."

Diane laughed. "Oh, I know you can take care of yourself. That's the problem with men. You think you've got everything taken care of. Well, let me give you a little womanly advice, Cal. Just when you think you've got it all figured out, that's when life tends to slap you in the back of the head." She paused, and her face softened, and she reached out her hand and stroked his cheek. "I love you, Cal. I want to spend the rest of my life with you, but if we can't keep the promises we make, I just... I can't..."

"What are you saying?"

"I'm not saying anything, Cal. I'm just talking. That's what couples do. They communicate." Diane's hand went back to her lap. "Now, are you going to tell me what happened?"

"Can I at least get a sip of wine first?"

"No. Tell me the story."

Cal exhaled and began the tale, leaving out nothing. Starting with finding the key at the Quinn's house, then meeting Corporal Edgerton, and finally about their interrogation of Lester Howe. Diane listened to it all, sipping her wine, nodding thoughtfully at certain points, her agile mind adjusting, turning, analyzing.

"So when we got back to the War Room," Cal finished, "Neil explained that he had gotten into the flash drive, but everything was still gibberish, in some kind of code. Apparently we need some kind of key to the code to decipher it."

"What kind of key?"

Cal realized that his girlfriend knew more about data bytes and secret codes than he did. A career in Naval intelligence will do that.

"That's where it gets interesting."

"Right, because up till now you've been boring the hell out of me." She had one eyebrow raised. She still wasn't happy, but at least they'd fallen into their old routine. Snark always helped lighten the room.

"This guy, Lester Howe, he said there's another flash drive and it's hidden in a safe in the basement of his father's office building. It's a place they call The Aquarium. How weird is that?"

"So let me guess. Your plan is to somehow break into a civilian office building, steal said flash drive, and figure out the mystery. It sounds like a bad episode of the Hardy Boys."

Cal had to literally bite his tongue to stave off his smart ass reply.

"You know what, you don't even have to answer that. I already know the answer." Diane drained the remainder of her glass in one swig and set it on the table. "Cal, how much longer do you think you can do this?"

For a second, Cal thought she was talking about their relationship. "You mean what I do for a living? I don't know. I hadn't really thought about it."

"But we've talked about it," Diane said, blinking slowly. "You said you were excited about taking 'a step back', as you put it. You said you wanted to find new adventures, to travel, that you'd never had time to taste the finer things in life. Remember? You said you've been working like a dog since you enlisted in the Marine Corps. Am I getting that right?"

Cal nodded. "That's right."

She took a deep breath and let it out slowly. "I just started a new job. We're just getting through that mess from Europe. I really want to give the Navy a shot. But Cal, I can't do that in good conscience if my boyfriend is running around playing James Bond all the time."

"I thought you said we were the Hardy Boys," Cal said with a half grin. "When did I get the promotion?"

Diane rolled her eyes. "You know what I mean. Give this to the authorities, Cal. Hell, give it to Brandon if you want. I'm sure he can sic the FBI on this Senator Fowler. Oh, and by the way, the fact that you have a prisoner in a supposedly private home in the middle of Charlottesville, you don't think that will raise any eyebrows?"

"He's technically in custody."

"I don't care what you call it, Cal. It's trouble, for you, for all your friends. Not to mention, it's trouble for *us*. And I won't even go into the fact that it was pretty convenient that your man in custody divulged that information. It looks to me like somebody's dropping the bread trail and you're just picking it up like Hansel and Gretel on their way to the candy house."

"At least tell me I'm Hansel and Daniel's Gretel," Cal said, trying to lighten the moment, but Diane's eyes went cold and she balled her fists in her lap.

"If we can't have one adult conversation, what am I supposed to think?"

Cal reached over and tried to grab her hand but she shook it off.

"Everything I've promised you is true," Cal said. "I love you too, but I have to do the right thing. Would you really have me just ignore this after someone attacked me?"

"Normal people go to the police or the FBI, Cal," Diane said, her body rigid. "You take the night to think about it." With this, she rose and walked off to bed.

It sounded like an ultimatum. They'd had their bumps in the past. The biggest had come after the death of his cousin, Travis Haden, when Cal simply disappeared. Diane had taken him back after that. Like any good Marine, he had his bone-head days, but there had been something in Diane's tone tonight. Maybe it was the way she looked at him, or the way her body was so rigid, her demeanor so resolute, that made the confrontation feel like *this was it*.

The two sides of Cal Stokes battled within him. There was the man who wanted to be the good boyfriend and maybe someday a good husband. And then there was the warrior, the patriot, the man who was not afraid to stare down death with his comrades. How could he possibly integrate both?

He sighed, refilled Diane's glass of wine, and sat back to think.

CHAPTER TWENTY-ONE

The man in the black utility uniform stepped into Senator Fowler's office and was about to say something, when he received the "Wait, one" signal from the senator, who was holding a piece of paper in his other hand and pacing about the room.

A speech, the man realized, and stepped dutifully to one side.

"And that is why, my fellow Republicans, we must stand with the president and ensure our nation's borders are protected..." he paused, scratching the paper with a pencil. "...*secure*... ensure our nation's borders are secure, ensure that our allies overseas are safe, and ensure that our men and women in uniform are given the respect and support..." he scratched again. "... respect and *care* that they deserve." The senator nodded to himself, set the speech on his desk, and then looked up at his guest. "How did it go?"

"Not well, Senator."

The squeaky clean uncle facade slipped as Fowler's eyes shot daggers at the man. But then, as quickly as it had slipped, his calm returned. "Talk to me."

"Sir, Howe's disappeared and left his rental vehicle behind... in public. It's on the wire, but only local news is reporting it. The police are calling it a drive-by shooting."

"Any witnesses?" the senator asked.

"One. A delivery woman who'd just arrived to restock the vending machines at the storage facility."

"Did she see our man?"

"No, Senator, but she did identify at least one other man. And by the description, I believe it was your Cal Stokes."

The senator turned toward the wall, his hands locked behind his back. "So, Lester Howe failed."

"I believe he did, sir."

"You believe so, eh? I'm assuming the police have the vehicle?"

"Yes, Senator."

"Very well... *pull it*."

That was all the man needed. He produced a phone from his pocket, punched in the code from memory, and pressed Send.

"Will that be all, Senator?"

"I never should have taken on Howe's boy. He was a simpleton at best. Remind me never to do favors like that again."

"Yes, sir," the uniformed man said uncomfortably, realizing, at the last moment, that the senator was probably just thinking out loud. He got his confirmation with an annoyed look from his boss.

"Should I get Mr. Howe Sr. on the phone, sir?"

"That won't be necessary. I'll take care of it. It's probably a blessing for him, anyway. Maybe Lester is dead, and Daddy won't have to babysit anymore."

"Yes, sir." The uniformed man nodded to his employer and left the office, all the while thinking that he detected something in the senator's countenance, something that he was holding back even from him. *He'll tell me soon enough*, the man thought, and then went back to his duties. There had been a lot of visitors in the last few days. If he didn't know any better, he would say the tide was turning.

———

THE POLICE STATION WAS QUIET, EXCEPT FOR THE RADIO next to the bored officer on watch and the clangs of the bars in the drunk tank. Officer William Nolan finished his inspection of the station and wrapped up by locking the door to the evidence room. He yawned and briefly contemplated going to the break room for another cup of coffee, his seventh of the day. But then he looked down at the brown bag in his hand that held the calzone he was supposed to be delivering to his pregnant wife. The sleepless nights were beginning to catch up with Officer Nolan. *Will it be this bad when the kid gets here?* he thought in his muddled mind.

He felt it his duty to pace up and down their first floor hallway with his wife as she soothed the baby in her belly back to sleep. Sarah said the baby was going to be a soccer player. Nolan secretly hoped it would be a boy and that he would play football. He himself had been a running back in high school, and his team had been decent enough to win districts. He was a diehard Redskins fan and never missed a game. He even had an eye on a baby-sized Redskins jersey that he was going to buy, no matter what Sarah said. He yawned again and was almost at the front door when he remembered.

Damn. He'd been in the middle of logging in the Hyundai from the shootout when she'd called, asking if he could bring home a calzone. "Extra cheese," she had said, "and with two sides of spaghetti sauce." So he did what any smart husband would do. He'd gone inside to make the call for the delivery guy. What he'd failed to accomplish in his sleep-deprived state was bring in the tablet he'd been using to log in the Hyundai. So now he weaved his way zombie-like through the impound lot, finally coming to the Hyundai.

The dash and the windowsills were covered in a fine black dust from where they'd swept for fingerprints, and every shell casing had already been bagged and tagged. There it was, lying on the front seat. The tablet with a big #4 stenciled on the back. It was one of five the department had received early that year. Luckily, he'd already taken pictures from every conceivable angle, inside and out. All he needed to do was log out and return the tablet to its docking station. The software would do the rest and he could go home to his perennially hungry wife.

Nolan grabbed the tablet and shoved it under one arm, closing the door carefully so as not to get any of the black dust on his hands. Then he stopped.

He heard something.

He looked to the fence line, but only saw cars driving by. No, it wasn't coming from out there. It was coming from inside... a long, slow *beep-beep, beep-beep, beep-beep...*

Nolan glanced at the tablet. It wasn't the mini-computer.

Then it sped up. *beep-beep, beep-beep, beep-beep...*

"Holy Christ," he yelled, dropping the tablet, but not the calzone. He bolted from the car.

Not more than five feet away.

Sarah... Redskins... the way she rubs her belly and smiles at him at midnight...

And the vehicle exploded.

CHAPTER TWENTY-TWO

The reporter from Sports Illustrated batted her eyes again. President Brandon Zimmer sighed. He was supposed to be talking about sports, his support for the Olympic team, and most importantly, his love for the New England Patriots.

While they touched on the summer games, the reporter seemed to be more interested in finding out about him and playing out her little flirty act.

"So, as I was saying about the Patriots..." Zimmer said, steering the topic back to where it should be. The reporter straightened up as if she'd been caught cheating in school, and he was about to tell her that she could relax when his secretary poked her head in the door.

"Call for you, Mr. President. I have it waiting for you in the other room."

'In the other room' meant the reporter could not hear the coming conversation.

"If you'll excuse me, I'll be back in a couple minutes."

"Take your time, Mr. President. I'll just be lounging in the Oval Office."

Zimmer forced a smile. She was really laying it on thick. "Well, don't steal the ashtrays. They were a gift from the Prime Minister of Sweden."

When he stepped out of the Oval Office, his secretary gave him a heavily encrypted phone that only had one use: to talk to the men of the Jefferson Group. While the president had been meaning to call Cal just to catch up, a phone call could only mean one thing: bad news.

"I'll take this, but then when I come back, can you make sure we stick to the schedule?"

The secretary took his meaning and smiled. "A little forward, Mr. President?"

"That she is." Then he went to find a quiet spot to chat. "Hey, Cal."

"*I hear you're talking to a reporter from Sports Illustrated. Are they putting you on the cover of the swimsuit edition?*"

"Very funny. I wish it were about that. Do you ever get the feeling that reporters are just trying to weasel their way in for a juicy scoop, or get you to say something you shouldn't? Like, yeah, JFK still lives downstairs. He's got a room with Jimmy Hoffa."

Cal chuckled. "*That game is all yours, Mr. President. I'm just a lowly soldier out here trying to find my way.*"

"So, what's going on? Is everything okay? How's Liberty doing?" Liberty was Cal's German short-haired pointer. She'd been injured in a terrorist attack in Paris, smack dab in the middle of a crowded train station.

"*She's wagging her tail in a rehab facility in West Virginia. They say she's doing a lot better. I get to pick her up in a couple weeks.*"

"That's good to hear," Zimmer said. "I'd like to see her, if that's possible. She is the hero of France after all. Boy, how the French President liked to talk my ear off about that one. You know how hard it was to pretend I didn't know who Liberty was or who her owner was?"

"Yeah. I don't know how you do it. Anyway, listen, the reason I called... how well do you know Senator Warren Fowler?"

"From Wisconsin. The Chairman of the RNC. I know him very well. Good man. He really helped garner support from the Republicans after the McKnight affair. Why do you ask?"

There was hesitation on the other end.

"What's up, Cal?"

"What if it turned out Fowler wasn't as good a guy as you thought he was?"

Zimmer's stomach turned. Was this another fox in the henhouse? "Tell me," Zimmer said, his voice having gone flat. Going into his second term as president, Zimmer was used to bad news. And yet, it was painful to consider that someone he and most Americans admired was not who everyone thought he was.

"I'm really not sure where to begin."

"Just give it to me, Cal."

Cal exhaled, and then proceeded to explain everything that had happened in the preceding days. The crash, the chase, and the supposed connection to Senator Fowler.

"And you're sure about this?" Zimmer asked when Cal had finished.

"I'm not really sure about anything. I was hoping you could give me some insight into this guy."

"This *guy* is the Mr. Rogers of Washington," Zimmer said. "He's squeaky clean. If ever there was a politician who didn't act like a politician, it's Warren Fowler."

"That's what makes him all the more dangerous. Brandon, we need to find out if—"

"Wait a minute. Hold on. Have you done anything to look into his connection with this bizarre string of events?"

"Not directly," Cal said.

Zimmer needed to think. He and the men at The

Jefferson Group had agreed to cease all operations for the time being. Part of it was that the men deserved the break, but secretly, Zimmer feared that his connections with the covert group would soon be uncovered.

"Do you think he knows about our arrangement?" he said.

"*That's what I'm worried about. This could be another McKnight in the making.*"

"Christ, Cal. What am I supposed to do with this? I can't just go knock on the man's door and say, 'Hey, Warren. You know this sketchy Marine who died? And, oh, by the way, are you trying to kill my best friend?'"

"*I'm not asking you to do that. I just thought you should know what's going on in case things get—*"

"Out of hand?"

"*I was going to say complicated.*"

"Is there ever a time that things aren't complicated with you?"

Cal chuckled again. "*It's funny you say that. Diane pretty much told me the same thing last night. Had to sleep in the doghouse because of it.*"

"I'm sorry to hear that. Is everything okay with you two?"

"*Let's just say she's on your side on this one.*"

"I knew I liked that girl," the president said. "She's pretty special, Cal. Hang on to her."

"*Yeah, I'm trying. Say, you just gave me an idea. You think it would be possible to get the FBI to look into Fowler?*"

Zimmer closed his eyes. Siccing the FBI on a member of the opposing party, one with a sterling reputation no less, would definitely get complicated. This was dangerously close to Nixon territory.

"I think I've got someone who can keep it quiet," Zimmer offered, albeit reluctantly.

"*Okay, thanks. You'll let me know what you find out?*"

"Sure, but Cal..."

"*Yeah?*"

"Try to keep the collateral damage to a minimum. Please? I'd really like to start my second term at the White House on a positive note, if you don't mind."

"*I have no idea what you're talking about, Mr. President. This Marine likes to color inside the lines.*"

As the president hung up the phone, the disturbing thought that echoed in his mind...

His friend Cal Stokes had never met a line he wouldn't cross.

CHAPTER TWENTY-THREE

"Man, am I glad we installed that safe room," Gaucho said as he walked into the kitchen following the scent of sizzling bacon. "It doubles nicely as a jail cell. I'd go nuts if I had to watch that guy day and night."

Top was at his customary spot, making eggs to order, and doing final prep on his mama's famous biscuits. His Johnson & Wales education was put to good use for the men of the Jefferson Group.

He brushed the tops of the biscuits with a wash of cream and black pepper. "What are you babbling about now, boy?"

"I was just saying that I hate watching prisoners. It's either boring as hell, or you got to stop a guy from slitting his wrists or trying to choke himself with his own tongue."

"Lester give you any trouble?"

"No, he's been pretty good. Said he wants to talk to a lawyer."

Top snorted. "I'll see if I can get one out of the yellow pages."

"Yeah, but man, what are we going to do with him? We're

not built for this. We've got to give him to someone at some point, right?"

"Gaucho, my friend, why don't we think about it, as you regale your belly with the power of Mama's biscuits and a heaping helping of my famous scrambled eggs?"

"You better put some bacon on there, too."

"Don't you worry. I made a new friend with a farmer out in Albemarle County. Check these babies out." He held up a piece of bacon that must have been half-inch thick. "Maple-wood smoked."

Gaucho's mouth watered. "Alright. Give it to me."

When Gaucho was halfway through his food, and watching their prisoner between bites on the small, baby monitor-type screen, Cal and Daniel walked in.

Gaucho made a sound like a trumpet. "Hear ye, hear ye. The Marines have arrived."

Daniel surprised him by giving him a half-bow.

"Looks like Snake Eyes woke up on his right side of the bed today. You, on the other hand, Cal, look like you could use a GI shower."

"Yeah," Cal said, running a hand over his face. "I didn't get much sleep last night."

"Trouble in paradise?"

Cal gave him a look as if to say, "Please don't ask."

"Well," said Gaucho, shoveling a forkful of eggs into his mouth, "our friend in the basement has eaten his protein shake breakfast. He's gone to the lavatory and is now playing the role of perfect brig bunny. Speaking of which, you have any idea what we're going to do with that guy?"

Cal shook his head, then walked over to the coffeepot and poured himself a steaming mug of gourmet Kona blend. "I just got off the phone with Brandon. He's going to have someone at the FBI look into the Fowler thing. And no, I have no idea what we're going to do with Lester."

"Lester," said Top, peeling open a steaming biscuit. "I mean, who names their child Lester? I thought that name went out of fashion back in the 50s."

"It's probably a family name," Gaucho suggested.

"I thought rich daddies gave their baby boys names like Thurston or Richmond."

"Speaking of Lester's dad," Daniel said, "Neil and I found the place Lester was talking about, The Aquarium."

"Please tell me it isn't in Roanoke," Cal said.

"It's actually in Wisconsin," Daniel said.

"Worse," Cal grumbled. "There's probably three feet of snow on the ground right now." He took a healthy swig of coffee.

"Actually only a foot," Daniel said matter-of-factly.

"I stand corrected." He made the 'give it to me' gesture.

Daniel continued. "The Aquarium is actually a government facility. Lester's father, Robert Howe, built it a couple years ago. He keeps an office in the lower levels."

"Is there good news to this story?"

"Oh, it has the usual, 24-hour security, state-of-the-art surveillance system."

"Man, that's just another damn day in the park for you," Gaucho said, pointing at Daniel with a fork. "Ol' Snake eyes will go right up in there, tell them who he is, and they'll give him a private tour of the place, complete with champagne and strawberries. Either that or he'll dress up in a ninja suit and slip in through a crack in the wall."

Daniel smiled. "I didn't even get to the best part yet. Turns out Senator Fowler also has an office in the building and get this, right next door is an office sublet to The America Institute."

"Well, that's perfect," Gaucho said. "We've got everybody sitting in one place. With Brandon on our side, I say we round up the troops, dig out some marshal badges or maybe borrow some from the FBI, then march in there and take what we want."

"It's not going to be that easy," Cal said. "Brandon is hesitant about us doing anything."

"Oh, come on," said Gaucho, throwing a balled-up napkin at him. "Are you talking about that time off? I'm sick of time off. I'm ready to get back to work."

"Seems like you and I are the only ones on the same page. Even Daniel here says we should hand it off to the Feds."

"Hey, don't you throw me in that boat," Top said, handing Cal a plate of food. "Wherever my Mexican brother goes, I go, especially if there's snow involved. I love to see the look on little Gauchito's face when he has to trudge through snow."

Gaucho shivered. "Right, I forgot about that. Well, at least it's an office building and not some godforsaken mountain in Wyoming.

Top was just heaping the rest of the meaty bacon onto a platter when his phone on the counter buzzed. "Hey, Gauchito, do you mind getting that? My hands are covered in bacon grease."

"Sure." Gaucho slipped off the bar stool and went to grab the phone. "It's Edgerton." Gaucho read the text and his eyes narrowed. "He said there's been an explosion at the Roanoke Police Department. One officer was killed."

Top looked at him. "What has that got to do with us?"

"It was Lester Howe's car," Gaucho said. "The Hyundai he tried to take Cal and Daniel out in. Edgerton says it's all over the news up there. He confirmed with a buddy on the force that it was the same car."

"Okay," Top said, "what the hell does that mean?"

It was the ever astute Daniel who answered. "It means whoever sent Lester Howe to kill us is now covering their tracks."

The men were suddenly not so hungry.

CHAPTER TWENTY-FOUR

The look on Lester Howe's face said it all. He hadn't known about the explosives rigged to the undercarriage of the car. "I don't understand," he sputtered. "They gave me the rental. I don't know why they put it there."

"It's called insurance, Lester," Gaucho said. "Apparently, they thought you were a liability. Or, at least, there was a chance that you could be."

"But the senator is a good man, and he knows my father. They're friends. My dad is the one that got me the job."

"Maybe your dad doesn't like you as much as you think," Cal suggested.

"No, that's impossible. He helped me when I came home."

"Well, they have an interesting way of showing they care. Didn't it raise any questions when they gave you a Hyundai and not some more expensive vehicle?

"I just thought they were cheap."

"Well now," Cal said, "unless I'm mistaken, it seems as though you're on our side now, Lester."

Lester stared down the floor, his head moving back and

forth, like he was having some kind of internal conversation, trying to make sense of the situation. "Impossible," he said under his breath. Then the head shaking stopped, and he looked up at Cal. "What do you want to know?"

"Tell me how we can get into your father's office."

"That's impossible. Security is tight."

"You let us take care of that. Now, what about this other flash drive? What do you think is on it?"

Lester's jaw was set as if he'd made up his mind. "It has to be Operation Neptune Spear."

"What is Operation Neptune Spear?"

"I don't know everything. I just heard pieces of it. They ran it out of my dad's office, but it was the senator who was behind it. I'm pretty sure there were weapon shipments, and laundering of money to pay for them, that kind of thing. I heard some things, and it was easy to see when shipments were coming in and going out. I never got to see inside the trucks, but I always assumed what was in them."

"What was it all for?" Daniel asked.

"I don't know. Like I said, they never told me anything. I was brought in to take care of you guys. If Tommy had followed through I wouldn't even be here right now."

"How well did you know Tommy Quinn?"

"I only met him a couple of times. I mainly knew him by reputation."

"And what was his reputation?" Daniel said.

"They said he was the kind of guy who took the jobs that nobody else would take. They said he was reckless, but he always got the job done. Obviously that all changed a few days back. Everyone was told to cease contact with him and not to ask why. But you know how it is. Rumors get around. They said he broke protocol or something. I was confused when I first heard about it, to be honest."

"And why is that?" Cal asked.

"Tommy was a star. I'd even heard the senator talking to my dad about him, about how special he was. I mean it really sounded like he was talking about his own son."

"And what happened after Tommy died?"

"They passed the word that if anyone talked to the police or the authorities about Tommy, they would be prosecuted."

"I don't know, Cal," Top said. "This whole thing seems awfully convenient. Why would Tommy have access to that type of information, something that could take the senator down?"

Cal pursed his lips and thought. So many things didn't make sense at the moment. And there was, of course, Diane's voice in the back of his head saying that he should back off. *Give it to someone else. Let the FBI handle it.*

But whether it was because he felt responsible for the Quinn family now, or that he was trying to salvage the reputation of a fellow Marine, or maybe he just wanted to root out a corrupt senator; whatever the reason, Cal knew he couldn't let it go. Maybe it was all of those things tied up in one messy ball of yarn.

Lester scowled. "They brought me in to clean up the mess. That's what the senator called it."

"But why you?" Cal said. "If you mind me saying, Lester, you don't seem like you're very good at the job. You folded five minutes into our first conversation. It seems more like you're the patsy than a solution to any problem."

Lester's face reddened and he clenched his fist, tugging against his bonds. "I was a good soldier. I was trying to be a good son. I followed the senator's lead. I guess I'm a poor judge of character, I don't know. He took advantage of me. They both did. I tried to ignore it for a long time. My father... he's always been embarrassed with me. He was a war hero, you know, staying in Vietnam after everyone else left. He saved a lot of lives. I was going to be like him and I tried."

Lester's body slackened and his expression was now one of defeat. "You should have seen the look on his face when I came back from Afghanistan, broken, beat down. He told me I was weak. But I'm his only son, so he did his duty as a father." The last word came out sour, like a curse. "So there it is. You know the truth. I'm an embarrassment. The first chance I get to redeem myself and I screw it up. What do you want me to say, that I was wrong? I can still help you if you let me. You don't have to trust me, but I can give you whatever information that might help. Check it out if you want, but just give me a chance. That's all I ask."

"That's a funny request coming from someone who just tried to kill me."

Lester stared down, breathing heavily through his nose.

Top broke in. "Maybe Neil can get in there without us having to go in physically."

"We already floated that. He said aside from going in and planting Trojan software, he's flying blind."

"I could get you in," Lester said, his eyes bright now.

"You're the one that said we shouldn't trust you."

"So don't. Rig me with something, explosives if you want. Put a hidden camera on me so you know what's going on. I can come up with a story, some kind of excuse for why I had to disappear. I could be in and out in no time."

"It's not a bad idea," Top said.

"It's definitely doable," Gaucho said. "I bet Neil could rig up something that would be really hard to detect."

"What do you think?" Cal asked Daniel.

"If it doesn't involve us going in, I think it's worth a shot."

Cal chuckled incredulously. "I can't believe you guys are considering this."

"Cal, you know my position," Top said.

"Yeah. Me too," added Gaucho. "Something about this doesn't smell right, man. Let Lester go in. If he proves himself, then we're all good. If he screws it up, well, then, we're no further away from the solution than we are right now."

Cal couldn't disagree. The men in the room were anything but cowards. Maybe they were right. Maybe Diane was right. Maybe it was time to dump Lester in the laps of the FBI. Let them untangle Fowler's web.

No.

It was personal now. They'd come after him and his friends. They'd left the Quinns without a son. Cal would not leave the matter to someone else.

"Okay, let's do it. Lester goes in. Tell Neil I want him rigged with every high-tech monitoring device he can get past security."

"And what happens when this is over?" Lester asked. "What will you do with me?"

Cal looked him in the eye. "We'll just have to wait and see. Let's put it this way: you're not really in any position to negotiate."

CHAPTER TWENTY-FIVE

Corporal Edgerton rang the doorbell of the impressive two-story residence. He'd never been to such a nice house. He came from a working class family that was tight-knit in the way that many immigrant clans that arrived in the United States in the early 1900s were. During the preceding century, his family slowly made its way from New York over to Boston, down to Philadelphia, and splintered off from there.

Edgerton's parents had arrived in Roanoke just in time for the birth of their only son. As far back as he could remember, his father wanted him to learn a trade. Maybe he'd spend the rest of his days as an electrician or a general contractor. His mother had wanted him to stay in school and be the first in the extended family to earn an undergraduate degree.

He had not excelled in school, much to the chagrin of his mother. It wasn't because he couldn't learn, or that he wasn't bright. It was because of his small stature and his shyness. He was an easy target. He learned from his first days in middle school that it was better to stay with what friends he had and try to stay out of the limelight, than to be endlessly tormented by the roving groups of bullies in his middle and then high school. He knew, even as his classmates walked across the graduation stage to be presented with their honors' sashes and valedictorian accolades, that he could easily have been one of them if he had chosen differently.

It was a wakeup call for young Bryan. That same night, without his mother and father knowing, he went down to the Marine recruiting office and volunteered to go to boot camp at the earliest opportunity. The staff sergeant who'd explained all the formalities told him that he only had a reservist slot, and that if he wanted active duty, he'd have to wait at least two weeks to leave. Edgerton did not want to wait, so he signed up for the reserves, thinking that maybe it would be some consolation for his parents.

It wasn't.

When he arrived at home wearing his USMC T-shirt the staff sergeant had given him, and bearing a stack of papers that explained everything he was about to encounter at Parris Island, his mother had been furious.

"Don't you remember that boy down the street that died? He was in the Army too!"

He wanted to tell his mother that that boy's name was Paul, and that he'd died because he'd had too much to drink and decided it was a good idea to get behind the wheel to get back to his barracks. He had not died serving his country in some faraway land.

"And so now you want to leave us and you want to die too?" she said. "Why don't you just put me out of my misery now." His mother had actually walked to the kitchen and come back with a knife. "Here, take this. Cut out my heart. After everything we've done for you!"

Bryan had been in complete shock. His mother had always been a mild mannered woman, always sure to have dinner waiting for her husband and her son's lunch for his day at school or when he went to work at the video store on the weekends. Now, her true Irish temper showed. He remembered looking at his father for help, but the man just sat there with arms crossed.

He escaped to his room and lay awake until an hour before sunrise. He packed a few belongings, then went downstairs to write a note for his parents. It said simply, "I hope you guys come to graduation. I love you. - Bryan"

He left. His next stop, Parris Island.

Young Bryan Edgerton didn't know what to expect. He'd never seen *Apocalypse Now* or even *Full Metal Jacket*. His only exposure to Marines had been at his high school where a series of recruiters had made it a point to be at football games and other events where students would congregate. But he never once talked to them until he'd signed on the dotted line.

Now something miraculous happened when he rushed off the bus and onto the famed yellow footprints with the rest of the recruits. Everything else fell away: his missed opportunities in school, the lack of support from his parents, the mediocrity of his family. For some reason, when those drill instructors started yelling at him, Recruit Edgerton *smiled*. It, of course, elicited a stream of colorful strict description, but Recruit Edgerton didn't care. He looked straight through it and bit his tongue to keep from smiling.

Whether it was the darkness of the early morning drop off, or the brothers standing all around him, or maybe it was the way that the grass was manicured to perfection and every line around him seemed to be clean and orderly, Recruit Edgerton finally felt at home.

It wasn't that boot camp was easy. Far from it. Being one of the smallest came with its challenges, but he learned that what he lacked in size and strength, he more than made up for in brains and sheer determination. The rest of his platoon knew by the third week that they could always come to Recruit Edgerton if they needed help with their studies, with getting that perfect crease in their bedsheets, or just a friendly word of support.

When graduation day came and his parents had not made the journey to see him, he was disappointed. It would be months before he would see them again. But he contented himself with the fact that he'd finally found his calling and that he'd finally figured out who he was. He was a Marine, plain and simple. He had always been. All that was needed was for someone to give him a chance - to pull back the shell of his cocoon life and dig out his honor, courage, and commitment. Corporal Edgerton knew he would live by them until the day he died.

Like now, for example. It was taking courage for sure, and maybe a little bit of recklessness, to do what he did. He'd made the trip south of his own volition, and more than once imagined what his superiors would say.

But when Master Sergeant Willie Trent opened the front door of The Jefferson Group headquarters and said with a wide smile, "Aw, hell, here comes trouble," Corporal Edgerton couldn't help but return the smile as his body flooded with the same exact feeling he'd encountered upon taking his first steps along those yellow footprints.

CHAPTER TWENTY-SIX

I t took the rest of the day to plan out the operation. By the time they went to bed, Neil had all his contraptions set up and tested. Not only would they have crystal clear audio, but they would also see everything Lester saw with high definition video. And just as their once-reluctant informant had suggested, he would be strapped with various layers of explosive material that Neil assured the team would go undetected to all but the most invasive of examinations. Lester's belt, the inserts in his shoes, and even the ring around his collar were rigged to explode, should the need arise. For his part, Lester took it stoically, steeling himself like a soldier as he was turned into a time bomb and barely batted an eye as the setup was explained piece by piece by Neil.

Once morning came, the team drove out to the Charlottesville airport where their private jet was waiting. TJG's usual pilots, the Powers brothers, were in England for some international cross-training. Their third pilot, an Army chief warrant officer, was accompanying Jonas Layton, the TJG CEO, on his travels. They had a backup pilot on call who wouldn't be privy to their operational requirements, other than the fact that they needed to get in and out of Milwaukee within the next twenty-four hours.

Other than some last minute arrangements for ground transportation, the flight in was uneventful. Cpl. Edgerton, who by now had been nicknamed 'The Kid' by Top, spent the flight acting as if flying in a multi-million dollar jet was no big deal. Cal couldn't help but chuckle when he looked over at the awed Marine. Did he himself look that green as a Marine Corporal?

Cal had at first been against the idea of Edgerton coming along, but The Kid could be damned persuasive when he wanted to be. In the end, it came down to a single line uttered by the new team member: "*I want to know why Tommy died.*"

That had been enough for Cal. Deep down he knew that, even though this was the only mission he was part of, Edgerton wouldn't say a word to anyone outside the tight-knit group. Like any good Marine, he knew when to keep his mouth shut and focus on the mission. In the end, it turned out to be a blessing that The Kid had come along for the ride. After further examination of the building from public records, Neil said it would be a good call to have someone on the inside with a device that would boost the signal from Lester's myriad devices. Without hesitation, Edgerton volunteered. Really, it made sense. As Lester reminded them, Fowler was at least aware of the names and physical descriptions of Cal and Daniel. Top and Gaucho were far too conspicuous in appearance, despite their collective protests. Neil was needed to run the computer surveillance and communications.

Cal didn't like sending Edgerton in alone, but again, the young Marine presented the solution: he would visit Senator Fowler's office and claim he was looking for a job. It turned out that Fowler was well known for his active support of military veterans, and he'd often go out of his way to personally make contact with local employers to help secure jobs for returning vets. It had been Edgerton who supplied that tidbit of trivia.

The beauty of Edgerton's plan was that it was dead simple. He could go in with his own identification and walk out free and clear when his request was submitted. He could milk the time if Lester was held for an extended interrogation. Hopefully that wouldn't happen.

Lester himself had concocted a story to get himself out of the building if needed. He would simply tell his father that he wanted to speak with the senator in person. Lester felt fairly certain that the senator would be at his farm outside of town and not at the office he kept in the building they would soon infiltrate. Lester would never make it to the farm of course, but by the time his father figured that out, Lester would be long gone, hopefully with the key code in tow.

The runway was clear, but three feet of snow was piled just off the tarmac when they landed.

"Have I told you how much I hate the cold?" Gaucho complained, letting out a body jiggling shiver.

"Yeah, yeah. Suck it up, buttercup," Top said.

The plane taxied to a private hanger, and when they pulled up, two blacked out SUVs and two compact sedans were waiting for them. Neil, Cal and Daniel would go in one of the SUVs and monitor the situation from the parking lot outside the office building. Top and Gaucho would go in the second SUV and provide roving overwatch. They didn't really expect any trouble on the outside, seeing as how they were going to a suburban office park. But you never knew. Better to be safe than sorry.

Lester would leave in one of the sedans first and head straight to his father's building, following closely after by Edgerton in the second sedan. The entire convoy rolled out in staggered increments. Fifteen minutes after he'd left, Lester radioed in to say that he'd made it to the building.

It had been agreed that he would turn off the tiny radio to go through security, and then turn it back on once he was inside. If there was a second search, he could easily turn it off again with a button on the cuff of his sleeve.

A couple minutes after Lester went off-air, a phone call came in from Edgerton.

"I'm here. I just parked. Anything else before I go radio silent?"

Neil had rigged the signal booster inside the phone Edgerton now carried. There was no need to take anything else but his person and his wallet for identification.

"Just remember," Cal told the young corporal, "If this thing goes sideways, you get home on your own. No need to stick around. You take off."

"Roger that," came the reply.

Cal wondered if Edgerton would, in fact, leave his new team members behind. Hopefully it wouldn't come to that.

The office building looked like it could easily withstand the harshest of Wisconsin winters, what with its bunker-style concrete reinforcements. And yet, its gleaming window and flashy trim still gave it the look of something modern, and recently built at that.

A couple minutes after Cal's vehicle arrived, Lester's video and audio feed came on. They watched as officers escorted him down a long hallway to a bank of elevators. Neither he nor his two escorts said a word. All Cal could hear was the clomping of boots on tile. Then they were inside the elevator, and one of the guards pressed the button for their lower level destination. A chime dinged, and the doors opened again. Another long hallway came into view just as the radio crackled. This time it was Top's voice that came over the line.

"Cal, we have a problem."

"What is it? Our friend just got downstairs."

"You're not gonna believe this, but Senator Fowler just strolled onto the premises. No joke. Just appeared, like he was taking an afternoon stroll. Cal, he's taking the back entrance into the building."

All Cal could do now was watch Lester's video, and hope that Fowler was going up to his office instead of down to the lower level.

CHAPTER TWENTY-SEVEN

On the second floor, sitting in the senator's modest waiting room, Corporal Bryan Edgerton listened to the radio chatter through the mini earpiece Neil had inserted in his ear with a pair of tweezers. He knew the senator had just arrived. Would he go up or down?

The senator's office manager had been kind enough, taking down his name, his hometown, and promising him she'd be back in a few minutes. Edgerton couldn't just up and leave. Sure, Neil said that there was still a good chance that they could see and hear everything without the young Marine being in the building, but Edgerton didn't want to take that chance. He had a mission. He had a part in the covert operation. So instead of excusing himself from the office, he set his jaw and waited.

His patience was rewarded, for a couple minutes after the announcement from Top that the senator was on the premises, the senator himself walked into his second floor office. He was casually dressed, jeans and work boots, with a heavy parka tucked under one arm. "Good morning, son," he said as he entered.

Corporal Edgerton jumped to his feet. "Um, good morning, Senator."

"Are you here to see me?"

Edgerton hesitated. There was nothing about the senator that would make him presume that he was some kind of megalomaniac. Everything about the man projected calm and understanding. Edgerton had never met a politician in his life, and for some reason, he just couldn't make his brain understand that this could be an evil man.

"Oh, no, sir. I've already been helped, but thank you."

"Corporal Edgerton was in the Marine Corps," said the office manager coming in from the back.

"A Marine, eh?" the senator said, brightening. "Were you active duty or in the reserves?"

"In the reserves, sir. Stationed out of Roanoke."

The senator searched his mind for a moment. "Ah, yes, 4th CEB, isn't it?"

That surprised Edgerton. It was as if the obscure detail had been snatched out of the air and presented to him like a dead rabbit.

"Yes, sir. I'm surprised you knew that."

"Well, son, if you'd been around the block as many times as I have, you would understand why I make it my business to know many random details about our nation's military. Speaking of which, I think I knew a young man from that unit. Let me see if I remember..."

Edgerton's insides froze, though he tried to keep his face calm.

"Oh well. I'll remember at some point." Now he turned back to his manager. "Is there anything I can do for the corporal?"

"The corporal is here for assistance in getting a job," the office manager said. She gave him a knowing smile, as if the senator took personal responsibility for every visit like this and it was her job to keep him running on the day's schedule. "I've got him in the system, Senator. But if you'd like to speak with him, you've got some time before your first meeting."

"Excellent. Corporal, how do you take your coffee?"

"Black, please, sir." Edgerton hoped the senator hadn't seen him gulp down his nerves.

"Janet, would you mind fetching us two cups, and bring them into my office. It's not every day we get a visitor from out of town, and a Marine to boot."

"Senator, I don't want to take up your morning," Edgerton said, bordering on desperation should he tip the senator off further.

"Nonsense, Corporal. I may not be in the Senate anymore, but I still see it as my duty to take care of the men and women defending this country."

"That's very kind of you, sir."

"Consider it settled then. I'm sure Janet has a few more questions for you. Let me get some things off my plate, and then why don't you come back and we'll chat. Sound good?"

"Yes, sir. Thank you, Senator." Edgerton smiled and shook the man's hand.

Janet the office manager came over and handed him a small stack of papers. When he looked down, he saw that it contained all the information he'd provided.

"Just sign where the sticky note is on page three. That's just saying that you would like the senator to speak on your behalf, and then that's it."

His mouth dry, Edgerton signed on page three and handed the stack of papers back to the kind woman. She looked at him for a moment. There was a twinkling of amusement in her eyes. "Corporal, I feel I should let you know that the senator's five-minute conversations frequently turn into two-hour pow-wows. I hope you don't have plans."

"Excuse me?"

"The senator meant what he said. If he has his way, he'll find out everything about you. He really is a good man, you know. Got me this job when I lost mine at the mill. There aren't many people in this town he hasn't touched. I suggest you just be yourself and enjoy your time with him."

"Yes, ma'am. Thank you."

"Oh, and Corporal?"

"Yes, ma'am?"

"Your phone." She pointed to where Edgerton had left his phone on top of a stack of magazines. "It's ringing," she said. "I'll come get you once the senator finishes returning his morning emails." She spun on her heel and returned to her duties.

Edgerton grabbed the phone, debating whether he should even bother taking the call.

"*We've got a problem,*" Cal said.

Luckily, there was no one in the room, but Edgerton was still wary about speaking openly. "Hey, man, what's going on?" He tried to sound nonchalant, but his words felt forced. He hoped Cal would pick up on his discomfort.

"*Your earpiece went out. We've been trying to call you.*"

"Okay, yeah, sorry about that." Edgerton could feel the sweat forming along his spine. Cal and his men were resorting to cellphone use, something that had been deemed the last option for communication. That meant things were going wrong. He could kick himself for not noticing the sound go out in his ear.

"I'm about to go in and see the senator. Do you want me to come home?" He said it just loud enough for Janet to hear.

There was a pause on the other end. "*No, no. Maybe that's better. See how long you can keep him occupied. I'll text you when Lester is clear.*"

Edgerton didn't know how to ask whether the booster he was holding in his hand was still working. Since Cal didn't mention it, he assumed that it was, and that it was imperative that he stay in the building.

"Okay, I'll take care of it and I'll see you soon."

The last thing Cal said before he hung up the phone was, "*Be careful, kid.*"

"Yeah, thanks."

The call ended. Edgerton took a seat. He knew he was a terrible liar. It was one of the reasons he'd suggested to Cal that he go in telling the truth. But now, the truth could be his undoing. Mentioning that he was with the 4th CEB out of Roanoke didn't spell complete disaster. Technically, Tommy Quinn had been part of the unit for a time to be closer to home on drill weekends. He'd spent most of his time in the Corps with a reserve infantry battalion out of Pennsylvania. That was where the two Marines had met, not in Roanoke.

Edgerton said a quick prayer that Fowler wouldn't put two and two together.

Seconds later, the office manager appeared again and said with a motherly smile, "Corporal, the senator will see you now."

CHAPTER TWENTY-EIGHT

"You think he'll be okay?" Daniel asked. He'd been listening to the phone call.

"I think he can take care of himself," Cal said. "Lester's the one I'm worried about."

He pointed to the monitor and the unfolding scene in the sub level of the office building. Lester had tried to explain to his father what had happened at the storage facility - that the cops had shown up and he'd run. But his father was having none of it. He was laying down the law, listing each and every single time Lester had failed.

"You're a disgrace. I give you a task. One. Simple. Task. And what do you do? You run and hide. If your mother was alive to see you, she—"

"Don't bring her into this," Lester snapped. "You want to talk about failure? Let's talk about you, Dad. How about the fact that you cheated on Mom, and that's what made her take her own life?"

"Oh, you're a fine lawyer, aren't you? Your mother killed herself because she was nuts."

"Knock it off, Dad. You know I'm right. She couldn't

stand the sight of you. You want to know who's weak? You want to know who's a failure? You, Dad. I've tried my whole life to prove myself to you. But you see, that's where I got it wrong. I understand that now, and I'm not going to be treated like a child anymore."

Cal figured this was the end. Game called on account of family drama. The so-called explosives Neil had strapped to Lester were just extra pieces of fabric. There had been no debate on that point. No man at TJG was savage enough to wire a weak-willed pawn like Lester with explosives. It was cruel and unnecessary. They'd decided, without telling Lester, that the only thing they would do if he got caught was kill the transmission and leave.

Daniel picked up the microphone that fed into Lester's earpiece. "Calm down, Lester. Talk to your Dad, but don't get him too riled up." Daniel's word had an instant effect.

"Dad, I'm no one's hero but my own. I never had to be. I... just wanted to give you and Mom the best part of me."

Robert Howe's face softened. "Look, son, I'm sorry I said what I said, but you have to understand, I'm under a lot of pressure here. The company, *our* company is struggling. If I don't figure things out quick, well, there won't be much of a legacy for me to leave you."

Lester didn't answer. He'd followed his father into another room. Cal could see pictures on the wall. Before and after snapshots of raw land developed into a massive industrial complex. Another showed the office building they were now casing.

"Look, I have a meeting upstairs in a few minutes. Why don't you make yourself comfortable, maybe order some food. We'll chat when I get back."

The excuse about going out to the senator's farm was long gone, considering the senator's current location, so Cal wondered what Lester would say. "Sure Dad, I'll hang out.

I've got some things to do in town. I might run out for a bit."

"Alright." The man took a few steps and turned. "You gonna be okay?"

"Do you still have that stash of Colonel E. H. Taylor in here?"

The elder Howe grinned and ducked behind a cabinet. He came out with a bottle of Kentucky's finest, Colonel E. H. Taylor bourbon.

"My last bottle. Maybe we can make a run down there sometime soon and see if we can't pry some out of the Master Distiller's hands." He said like it was something they had done numerous times before, cruising down to the bourbon trail, just father and son, laying out their vision for the future of the family company.

Robert Howe left the bottle on the table, patted his son on the shoulder, and then closed the door as he exited. Lester was all alone, so near to his goal.

"Now you know what I have to put up with," Lester mumbled to the men in the black SUV.

"Take your time," Daniel said. "We'll try to get you confirmation that your dad went upstairs. I don't want him to sneak up on you."

Lester nodded. He grabbed a glass from his father's wet bar and stepped over to the rare bourbon and poured himself a finger.

"You think that's smart?" Cal whispered to Daniel.

"He'll be fine."

The camera view shifted. Lester was now behind his father's desk. He rummaged through a bottom drawer, moving papers aside. Cal could barely see into the dark cavern.

Then it was there. A small safe. Lester quickly put in the combination and clicked it open. There was an assortment of valuables inside; some gold and silver coins, a wad of cash, and what looked like a stack of property deeds. Lester stuck his hand in, and it came out with a flash drive that he showed to the camera embedded in his third shirt button.

"Got it," Lester said. He then closed the safe and put the drawer in its prior position. Having moved back around the desk, he grabbed the glass of bourbon and sat down. "To you, Dad," he said, raising his glass. The glass came back down in full view of the camera. It was empty, and that was when the screen went blank.

"What the hell?" Cal said.

Three seconds later, an explosion rattled the office building.

CHAPTER TWENTY-NINE

dgerton had just reached for his cup of coffee on the senator's desk when he was thrown violently to the floor. A lamp from the desk fell, shattering twelve inches from his face, as the building swayed. Or maybe it was just his head swaying. He hit it hard coming down. Now, as he tried to focus, his vision blurred. He was seeing triple. The smell of drywall dust preceded the wail of alarms by a split second.

"Corporal, are you alright?" It was the senator's voice coming from the other side of the desk. Edgerton tried to get to his hands and knees, but a wave of nausea sent him back to the floor.

Breathe, he told himself. He had been knocked unconscious one time before. It was during the final push to reclaim an Afghan town that someone up on high had deemed strategic. To Edgerton, who was a lance corporal at the time, the place looked like a goat herders' paradise and nothing more. But they'd gone anyway, because that's what Marines did. As part of the combat engineer detachment supporting the infantry battalion going in, he'd been assigned to clear the way. He was hit by an IED, and his world spun then much as it did now.

Breathe, he told himself again. In and out, his breaths came. There were no aftershocks.

"Corporal, answer me, are you alright?"

Edgerton could just make out a shadow coming into view. He blinked twice and his vision cleared a bit. "I just hit my head, sir." The senator reached down and tried to help the Marine off the floor. "If you don't mind, I think I'll just lie here for a moment, sir." And then his stomach rebelled. "I think I'm going to be sick."

"It's all right. You take your time. You stay right here. Let me go and see what happened."

Edgerton wasn't sure how long it had been before the senator returned, but he had composed himself enough, back to a sitting position.

"Come on, son. I've got to get you out of here. The building's on fire."

With surprising strength, the senator reached down and hoisted him up. The Marine couldn't shake the irony of the situation. He'd come in to help take the senator down, and now the senator was saving his life.

"What happened?" Edgerton just managed to asked, thinking that maybe the explosives Neil had strapped to Lester Howe had gone off. Maybe Lester had turned to the other side again. No, that wasn't right. Cal said there weren't any explosives. Corporal Edgerton was having a hard time focusing on anything, so he settled on just moving one foot in front of the other as the senator dragged him out the door. They moved into waiting area. The office manager, Janet, lay crumpled on the floor, blood covering half her body. Edgerton pointed as if to say that they should help her, but the senator kept moving.

"She's gone. I already checked." They made it out of the

second door and into the main hallway. Without windows, the only illumination came from the emergency lights blinking white and red. They were accompanied by blaring alarms and screams of panic from every which way.

"Not the elevator," Edgerton managed to say, but he could feel the energy fading, his body going slack.

"You hold on now, Corporal," the senator's voice was fading fast in Edgerton's muddled brain. "We'll get out of here together."

———

TOP AND GAUCHO WITNESSED THE EXPLOSION THAT RIPPED off part of the pretty facade of the government office building. One second they'd been staring up at the windows of the senator's office, and the next, debris was raining down on the parking lot. And a moment later, curls of smoke wafted into the frigid winter air.

"What the hell was that?" Gaucho said. "You don't think...?"

"No, that couldn't have been Lester."

"What about the kid? You think that was the senator's office?" Gaucho pointed up and it took Top a few seconds to realize that no, it hadn't been the block of windows they'd been watching.

"I think it was The American Institute office," Top said. All the sudden there was a squawk of transmissions coming in over the radio. They had a police scanner on. That chattered away first. Multiple units called to the scene, acknowledged by four, five, six, and then seven squad cars. "Come on, we need to get to the other side of the building."

They arrived to mass chaos. Workers streamed out of the building. The first police car had arrived and was trying to take command, but it was only one cop. Top spotted Cal and Daniel in the growing crowd and waved.

"What the hell happened?" Top said when he joined them.

"I don't know, but we lost comms with Lester. I have no idea where Edgerton went. Did you see anything on the other side?"

"Just the explosion," Top said. "I'm 99% sure it wasn't the senator's office, but I am equally sure that it was The America Institute."

"We need to get in there," Cal said.

He didn't have to tell the others twice. The four warriors rushed to the doorway, pushing through the stream of shocked workers trying to get away from the catastrophe.

The only police officer on the scene was yelling for them to move back. The Jefferson Group men ignored him, still pressing forward. They tried to be gentle as they slipped through the others, swimming against the tide. Top couldn't help but be amazed at the number of people coming out.

Top was about to apologize as a man slammed into his chest. Momentarily dazed, Top looked down to make sure the man was okay, and his eyes went wide.

"Lester?"

The turncoat looked up at Top. "I've got it. It's in my pocket."

Top had to yell over the roar of the police sirens that had just arrived to get Cal's attention. He pointed down at Lester.

"Get him out of here!" Cal yelled back.

Top nodded, motioned to Gaucho. The three men ran back to the second SUV.

———

The first floor had all but cleared out. There were few stragglers as Daniel and Cal entered the building, but no one who looked like they needed immediate medical attention. The first body they encountered was the security guard just behind the metal detector. Daniel bent down to examine him and the streak of red running down his face.

"He's been shot."

Shot? What the hell? Cal thought. "Come on. We've got to find Edgerton."

The farther they went into the building, the cloudier it got. Daniel flicked on a flashlight and led the way to the stairwell. They were almost there when the building shook again, ceiling tiles falling from above.

"We've got to hurry," Cal said. They were running now. They made it to the stairwell, but as soon as they opened the door, they were greeted by a gush of smoke.

"I can't see anything," Cal said. "Do you think he made it out?"

"I don't know, but we have to check," Daniel said. "I ain't about to leave a young Marine behind."

"I'm with you. Let's head up to the second floor, but we get out as fast as we can."

They never made it to the second floor. Halfway up the landing, they found a form slick with blood. It was Edgerton. Daniel moved to check him. "He's still breathing, but his pulse is weak."

That's when Cal heard the moaning.

"Give me a flashlight."

Cal moved further into the darkness, slipping part of his T-shirt over his nose and mouth. His eyes were burning now. He could feel the heat from the fire above. He saw a shape covered in rubble. It was a man, and he was moaning. It wasn't until he bent down, that Cal saw who it was: Senator Warren Fowler. His eyes were wide, but Cal could tell by the look of him that he was not seeing the man standing over him.

Great, Cal thought. Maybe the smart thing to do was leave him. No. A shred of doubt concerning the senator's connection to Tommy Quinn, and the overwhelming sense of doing the right thing made Cal scramble to dislodge his supposed enemy from the debris.

Cal heaved a steel girder away, then spent a few long moments pushing chunks of concrete away. The intensity of the growing fire urged Cal to move faster. Finally, the senator's body was free. Cal pulled him out, and the older man screamed in pain. Cal couldn't tell in the darkness, but he was sure that the man's leg was shattered in multiple places. Fowler screamed again.

"Hold on," Cal said, hoisting the man into his arms. Then, before he could think about it, he followed Daniel, who was carrying the unconscious Corporal Edgerton down to the first floor.

CHAPTER THIRTY

Due to its status as a government facility, reports about the office building in Milwaukee were sketchy and varied as they hit the news wire. Some sources said it was a gas leak, others an electrical fire, and still another said it was a disgruntled worker with a grudge who'd tossed a match into the gas room. The eyewitness accounts streamed in soon after, all describing an explosion. None had seen it, but they'd heard and felt it. Experts weighed in as the media snowball rolled downhill. By the time prime time news aired that night, it had gone from an event covered by two local news stations to a nationwide media circus, complete with hysterical speculations.

A report that a band of terrorists was seen storming the building was recanted by ABC News. One passerby interviewed on CBS said he saw an airplane, a small one, but still an airplane, crash into the building. Others thought that maybe it had been an explosive-laden drone that had done the damage. Everyone thought they knew the truth.

As night fell, so too did news outlets descend on the scene of eleven confirmed deaths and fifty to sixty wounded.

Then, just before ten pm on the east coast, NBC News said it had acquired surveillance video from authorities showing the office lobby minutes before the explosion.

And so with the rest of America, Cal Stokes and the rest of The Jefferson Group staff in Milwaukee, watched as a nondescript man carrying a briefcase walked into the lobby of the office building, his back to the camera, and hand identification to the security guard. The guard took it, examined it, and then the man in the suit pulled out a silenced pistol, shot the guard, and kept walking. The video fast-forwarded from there. The NBC News reporter called attention to the time-stamp, which indicated that it was some nine minutes later when the explosion rocked the building.

Cal muted the hotel room television. "Who do you think it was?" he asked the room.

Neil, Gaucho and Daniel were arrayed in various chairs. Lester Howe was asleep in the adjoining room. He'd emerged from the office building excited that he'd completed his mission, but the adrenaline had quickly worn off when he'd realized that his father might have been killed in the blast and that his part might finally be over. Top kept an eye on the exhausted man.

"I think we can rule out the senator," Daniel said.

Gaucho raised his hand. "I didn't want to say anything while Lester was here, but what about his dad? What if he did it?"

"He has motive," Cal said. "Remember when he was talking to Lester, he mentioned something about his company struggling. Maybe this was a plot to get insurance money or maybe the senator double-crossed him."

The news report flashed a banner on the bottom of the screen: Robert Howe was still missing in action.

As for the wounded, Cal had handed off Fowler to the emergency responders. There hadn't been a choice. The police recognized the politician as soon as Cal emerged from the building. Unfortunately, soon after they'd departed, the senator suffered a heart attack on the way to the hospital. President Zimmer had presented that detail in an earlier call. Senator Fowler was now lying in the ICU.

Daniel had taken the ambulance ride with Corporal Edgerton, with the others following behind. The kid was in stable condition, although the doctor said he'd suffered a severe concussion, something that could plague him for years. Daniel had asked the doctor if the young Marine could be moved, maybe taken back to Virginia to his parents, but the doctor had flatly denied the request. Daniel had left it at that and promised to be back later.

"Neil," Cal said, "are you any closer on cracking the flash drive?"

Other than monitoring various news sources, Neil had been working nonstop to try to meld the key code Lester had obtained from his father's office to the flash drive left by Tommy Quinn.

"I think I'm almost there, but then again, I thought the same thing two hours ago. Just when I think I'm in, another decryption starts running."

"Are you sure it's not a trick?" Gaucho asked. "Like maybe it's running a hidden program, and they're tracking us?"

Neil looked up and fixed Gaucho a hard stare. "You really think I'd fall for that?"

Gaucho shrugged, "Hey man, just trying to help. We'd all really like to know what's on that thing."

Neil's face brightened as he raised his hands in the air. "Whoa, whoa, whoa, hold on, I think I've done it. Yes! There it is." The others crowded around, but Neil shooed them to a proper distance. "Okay, let's see. Well, that's unexpected."

"What are you seeing?" Cal asked. He couldn't make out

the jumble of data filtering across Neil's screen. It looked like a scene from the Matrix.

"Right there. Don't you see it?"

"None of us see it," Daniel said.

"Oh, right." A few keystrokes later and the screen cleared. "There. Do you see it now?"

"Neil," Cal said, his patience at its limit, "all I see are a bunch of coded entries. Would you mind telling us what you see?"

"I really should put you guys through a coding class. I mean, this is really basic stuff. So, we were expecting like this big data dump, right? Like hundreds, maybe thousands, of files. I don't know. We talked about shipments and transactions. Hell, I don't know. I was hoping to maybe find out who shot JFK."

"Neil!" Cal barked.

"Right, right. Sorry. So here's the deal. There's none of that. There are two small files, Word files, nothing fancy."

"Can you open them?"

"Can't you see that I'm working on that?"

Cal had assumed that Neil's first declaration meant that he had full access now.

"Okay look, right here and right here." Neil pointed to two different jumbles of letters and numbers. "NP and MW, those are the files."

"What does that mean?" Gaucho asked?

"It means the decryption is still working. Why don't you guys go back to watching the news and I'll let you know when it's done."

Cal met Daniel's eyes and the sniper shook his head with a grin. Cal exhaled and went to his previous position across the room.

He had just sat down again when Neil said, "Never mind, I got it."

The crew converged once more. Cal was just within view of the laptop screen again. Everybody froze. Neil was so shaken that he almost dropped the computer off his lap.

"Are you seeing this?"

"Yeah," Cal said.

Right there on the screen was an official military photograph of a man they all knew, the man who had taken Neil's foot, the man who had killed one of Cal's best friends, a man they all thought was dead and long gone. The stern face of Nick Ponder, founder and CEO of the now defunct Ponder Group, a nemesis of not only Cal but of his father before him, stared at them with grimly determined eyes. It was a while before anyone spoke.

"Neil, what else is in the file?" Daniel asked.

Neil's hands shook as he tried to scroll down. He'd been tortured by Nick Ponder. Cal could only imagine what he was thinking.

"Here," Neil said, handing the laptop to Daniel.

Daniel took it in steady hands and repositioned himself so that the others could see. It was a very thorough dossier. It started with the usual name, hometown, mother's name. There was a complete school history, elementary up through college. The report listed every mission he'd ever been a part of in the military, and concluded his military service with a less than honorable discharge. A few lines later the dossier said that the dishonorable discharge had been upgraded to an honorable. It did not say why.

Next came a psychological profile of Ponder. Words jumped out at Cal: *Aggression... lack of empathy... violence...*

Cal had had no qualms about the man's death. He was a pure sadist, through and through.

The file took an interesting turn. It detailed government contracts procured by the Ponder Group. They skimmed through quickly, but Cal couldn't help but think that he detected a theme in the file, as if someone had been watching Nick his entire life and documenting every detail along the way. But why? Tommy Quinn couldn't have done that. Maybe he'd known Ponder years before.

They got through the first file. Cal was amazed that Ponder had accomplished so much in the private security world before his death. Sure, towards the end most of it had been illegal, but the breadth and scope of his accomplishments were impressive.

The next file was of a man none of them knew, Matthew Wilcox, son of Trisha Wilcox. No father listed. Hometown Baton Rouge, Louisiana. Wilcox's file did not start from childhood, but instead picked up at the age of 18 where he'd been accepted to LSU. Just like Nick Ponder, Wilcox had gone into the Army after college. While Ponder's career as a soldier had been marked with recklessness, Matthew Wilcox looked like the polar opposite. Awards, decorations, the file even included sterling evaluations from his superiors. He'd served six years, leaving with an honorable discharge and that was it. There was nothing else.

"Who do you think this Wilcox guy is?" Gaucho asked. "Maybe a friend of Ponder's?"

"No, this doesn't feel right," Cal said. He met Daniel's gaze.

"You know what we need to do," Daniel said.

Cal nodded. "We need to talk to Senator Fowler."

CHAPTER THIRTY-ONE

Senator Fowler blinked away the haze, annoyed that his customary ability to snap awake had somehow been snatched away by the heart attack. He blinked a few more times. Thought about ringing the call button. No, she would just fuss about him again, get him to move around in his bed and that would hurt.

He'd had a mild heart attack before. This one had been worse. His chest and head ached, he felt drained, but the pain in his leg helped sharpen his senses. He'd been in surgery most of the day, the doctor said. Fowler stopped listening when the doctor started explaining the third reconstruction. He knew it was doubtful that he would ever walk again. He didn't care.

His thoughts went to the young Marine he'd been talking to, the one he'd tried to save. Corporal Edgerton. He'd asked the doctors and nurses about the Marine, but no one knew where the young man had gone. They explained that the survivors of the blast had been taken to four different area hospitals depending on need. The senator had been told about the eleven deaths. He cringed. *It's all my fault,* he thought, but he wasn't one for self-pity. He hadn't made it to where he was in life by feeling sorry for himself or wallowing in a puddle of his mistakes.

No, he had to get out of the hospital and do something before more people were hurt.

"They say you're not going to walk again," came a voice from the shadows.

"Who's there?"

"Judging by your records, I doubt if you'll ever stand again."

The voice was not cruel. Just matter of fact. Stripped of all emotion.

"Come out to where I can see you." He wished he could flip on the overhead lights. That wasn't necessary as the man stepped into view and then recognition hit.

"Cal Stokes. How did you get in here?"

Stokes didn't look surprised that Fowler knew who he was.

"I have my ways. You don't remember, do you?"

"Remember what?"

"That I carried you out of the building."

Fowler's chest tightened. He winced and pushed the sensation away.

The senator narrowed his eyes. "They didn't know who you were, and I don't remember. You have no reason to lie about that. Thank you." The senator stared at him, unsure of where to start. "I'm sure you have questions for me."

"I do. You know it wasn't easy getting in here." He took a seat next to the hospital bed. "If I didn't know better, I'd say you're using your influence to keep someone out."

"You decrypted the files," Fowler said. It was the only reason the senator could think that Stokes would be so calm.

He'd been put through the wringer. Fowler had been part of that, so he braced for the worse.

"Yes, we got into the files, but we'll get to that soon enough. Tell me how you knew Tommy Quinn."

The mention of the name made Fowler's throat constrict. "I assume you know by now that he worked for me. Well, the story doesn't start there. You saw Nick's file, I assume?"

"I did."

Fowler exhaled. "I tried to help him, you know. Tried to steer him onto the right path, but he was hard-headed, just like his mother." He chucked sardonically. "I'm sure you know from experience that he had quite the mean streak. You saw the file. Harassing his superiors. Beating up his subordinates. Killing innocent civilians. I used to lie awake after hearing from him, thinking that maybe he was the devil incarnate, penance for my past."

He looked at Stokes. The man was confused.

"You haven't figured it out," Fowler said.

"Figured what out?"

"Nick was my son. I wasn't there when he was born, but I followed him throughout his childhood. Sent money to his mother. Tried to guide him from afar. When he got in trouble with the Army the first time, I felt it was my fatherly duty to step in. I was wrong. Nick took advantage of my position. Blackmailed me. Told me he'd expose our relationship. Since my wife was still alive at the time and I knew the revelation would crush her, not to mention my career, I went along with his plan.

"But, you know, a funny thing happens when you spend time with your child, even if your child is a man like Nick Ponder. I loved him, God help me. I'd always loved him. I helped him in any way I could. I funneled contracts his way. Helped cover up his indiscretions. I thought that maybe if I helped him one last time he would see the light. I was wrong, of course. But you know what the funny thing is? He's dead, rightfully, and I know of his long list of transgressions, and yet I still love him. Ain't that a kick in the head? He was my son by birth and by right. I never had a legitimate child. My wife wasn't ever able to bear children. Nick was... another chance to get it right."

Fowler stopped and stared at Stokes. He couldn't read the man's face. "You don't look surprised."

"Not much surprises me anymore, Senator. But I would like to know the rest of the story. Who was Ponder's mother?"

"No one of consequence. Just a pretty girl I met on the campaign trail. There were a lot of pretty girls. Sometimes it was a brunette. Other times it was a blonde with perky breasts, or an auburn beauty with a kind smile. There were so many I don't even remember half of them. Understand, I come from a different time. My father told me to see the world and sow my oats. He didn't want me to end up the way he did, so I dove headlong into politics. At that time, in the 70s, money and power mixed like a cocktail. Drugs, alcohol, and sex were added for a wonderful concoction of adventure and fun. I know you were just a child, but I'm sure you've read the stories of excess. I won't elaborate.

"And so that leads us to Matthew Wilcox. He was the sugar to Nick Ponder's salt. I never knew him as a child. I only discovered the connection when he showed up one day in my office in his military uniform. He was to be my military aide on Capitol Hill. I had no idea who he was, but he knew exactly who I was. He'd requested the assignment. Thanks to his exemplary career, he'd gotten the post. You should have seen him. All spit-shine and polish. I was taken in from the start. It wasn't until three months working together that he told me the truth. We'd had a little bit too much to drink, and he let slip that he was my biological son. I was momentarily shocked, but based on my past the shock didn't last. I tried my best to cultivate the relationship, but things soured. Months later, he left his post, submitting his papers and leaving the Army. I didn't hear from him for a good five years. Then one day I get a call from Nick. He called to say that The Ponder Group was full of Fowler's bastards. Matthew had joined their ranks. I was disappointed, to be sure. He had been a brave man. A kind soul. A natural leader. To see him thrown in alongside a misguided human being like Nick, well, it upset me more than you know.

"Fast forward a few years. I find out Nick is dead, killed on some mountain in Wyoming. I helped him get that land, you know. It was federal land. We procured the money, the agreement, and billed the place as an observation station. Well, he died, and I thought that Matthew perished as well. My life went into a nosedive. Not long before that I'd lost my wife, and then in one fell swoop I lost my two sons. I cannot tell you the depth of my pain. But I came out of it. I always have.

"Slowly, I put the pieces together. My informants brought me the information. Video from every hotel in the Jackson Hole area. We cut and pasted timelines, names and faces. I was obsessed. The scattered puzzle finally came together. Finally, it coalesced, right before the election this past November."

"You found out I killed Ponder," Stokes said softly.

Fowler nodded, his eyes narrowing again. "I was beyond furious. You'd torn my heart out. Stole my family. I didn't care what my sons had done. I wanted revenge. I dug further. I kept at it, crafting the perfect way to pay you back." Fowler sighed. "The more I dug, the more I found that you were what was right in this world. You were a bona-fide hero. You served with distinction. I've made plenty of mistakes in the past, but I am also a student of history. Grain by grain of sand, your life affected me. Then, as luck would have it, on one of those days, one of my bad days when my anger and my hatred of you overwhelmed me, pushing me down this dangerous path, who of all people should show up on my doorstep but Matthew Wilcox. I could see he'd changed. The understanding and kindness had left his eyes. He was a hard man now. Not like Nick. Not belligerent and boastful, but there was a quiet threat there. Not a cobra coiled and ready to strike. More like a trap door spider. He told me he was ready to come back, to work for me, to be together as father and son. And so, when I told him the truth of what had happened to Nick, he jumped in with both feet. First, I watched in wonder as he took control of the situation, dissecting you piece by piece, tracking your whereabouts, planning and scheming in ways that I had never even dared to think. I was ecstatic, and my doubts temporarily flew away in my insanity."

Fowler looked up and locked eyes with Stokes. "But then there came a day when my doubts returned. I couldn't ignore them any longer. I told Matthew that maybe we should step back. We could harness the power we'd made together into something more important, something that could mend our bond. We could protect our family and change the world." Fowler's words slipped away. He stared at the bed sheet. "He put a gun to my head and said, 'I changed one thing. I changed my attitude.' He said that if I told anyone, he'd kill me, and I would burn in hell knowing my son hated me for all eternity."

"So you went along just because of that," Cal said, his voice sharp with accusation.

"What else would you have me do? He was my son. I tried to find a way out. I helped you, didn't I? You've got the damn files. Now you know the link."

"You want us to do your dirty work." Stokes let out a

bitter laugh. "Because you couldn't keep your manhood in your pants years ago, my friends and I suffer? Oh, and not to mention Tommy and his parents. Then there are the people who died today. That's on you, Senator, not me."

Fowler sat up in bed, wincing at the pain. "Tommy was why I did it."

"Who was he to you? Another employee you could take advantage of like you're trying to do to me? No. I won't see anyone else harmed. The whole world will know soon enough what you've done, Senator."

Stokes rose. Fowler reached out and grabbed the man's arm. His chest was constricting again. He could feel another bout coming. The alarms from the monitors attached to his body went off, but he ignored them, staring up at the man that he had put all his faith in, to whom he'd given all his secrets. Stokes was his last chance. He was the only one who could fix it.

Fowler's words came out in a painful rasp. "I did it for Tommy and that's why Matthew killed him."

"Tommy died in a car crash. I saw it, remember?" Stokes glanced over at the monitor. It was beeping angrily now.

"You don't understand. Tommy was helping me, and Matthew found out. He threatened Tommy with his parents' lives. Tommy was helping me and he died because of me." Fowler's vision was blurring again but he could at least see that Stokes's face had softened.

"Don't worry, Senator. I'll take care of your son and it'll all be over."

Fowler shook his head. He could feel the darkness coming. "No, you have to know." He pulled Stokes closer. "I should have told him ... I should have told him what ... I should have told Tommy," Fowler gasped, clutching his chest.

"You should have told Tommy what?"

Somebody burst into the room then. It must have been a

nurse or maybe a doctor. Fowler couldn't tell. He ignored them. With all the force he could manage, he pulled Stokes all the way down so that he could whisper in his ear.

"I should have told Tommy that he was my son."

Then he drifted off into the darkness.

CHAPTER THIRTY-TWO

Officer Welch looked at his watch and exhaled in relief. *Time's almost up*. It had been a long night. He liked to volunteer for hospital guard duty because it was quiet. Officer Welch liked quiet. When he'd first joined the Milwaukee Police Department, he'd been ready to tackle the world. The only thing that had been tackled was him. A 350-pound pimp high on LSD had sent the rookie cop to the emergency room for thirty stitches and an arm cast. The pimp later told the judge that he thought Officer Welch was an alien. That was his first week on the job.

No, it was better to be sitting in a nice, quiet hospital than to be running around chasing criminals. Let the young pups do that. Welch was too close to retirement to be doing anything stupid.

He reflected back on the preceding hours with wonder. This duty should have been perfect. He had to keep an eye on none other than the famous Senator Warren Fowler, an icon of Wisconsin. The man was a champion for veterans" rights and a staunch advocate for police and first responders. Officer Welch was proud to be sitting outside the senator's door. It didn't hurt that there was more than one pretty nurse on duty, which made people-watching all the more fun.

Officer Welch's annoyances had ticked off in rapid succession. First the chief himself had called to say that there was a special visitor coming. The White House, of all places, had requested that an unnamed stranger be allowed to visit the senator.

"No name?" Welch had asked the chief. "How the hell am I supposed to know who he is?"

"I don't care. You figure it out, Welch. And don't forget, I still have your leave request on my desk. Don't screw this up."

Officer Welch had big plans for his final leave period. Without a wife or kids to tie him down, he'd booked a ten-day stay in Cancun. He'd drink the week away and see if he couldn't get a tan. He had no plans of screwing up between now and then. Welch knew the chief was just hanging the carrot over his head, and was just oblivious enough not to understand that the chief did it so that Lazy Jake, as the others called Welch behind his back, would actually do something for the rest of his time on the force.

The visitor was easy enough to spot. He wore a dark ball cap, shades and even flashed some official looking badge that Welch didn't recognize, and then strolled right in like he owned the place. *Hot shot*, Welch had thought.

That might have been the end to the story, but during the visitor's stay, a stay that did not include Officer Welch being in the room, alarm bells started going off. Doctors and nurses rushed to the senator's room and for a long terrifying moment, Welch thought that maybe the visitor had killed the senator. They would pin it on him, he thought irrationally, but then reassured himself that no, it had been the chief and the White House who had requested the private meeting. A private meeting meant that he could not be in the room, so really it wasn't his responsibility. He'd stacked up his rebuttals like a lawyer prepping to defend his capital murder case.

Then, to add to Welch's surprise, somehow, during all the commotion, the visitor had left, and now that Officer Welch thought about it, he didn't remember seeing the serious-looking man leave.

"It was not another heart attack," Welch heard the doctor say. "He's been under a lot of stress today. We'll have to do some more tests, but it was probably a panic attack. Give him point-five milligrams of alprazolam."

Now, as the minutes ticked by, Officer Welch couldn't wait to be off duty. His replacement would be coming soon. He wanted to call the station and make sure. Then, there he was walking down the hall.

"Hey, Matty, what do you say?"

Officer Matt Wilcox was everything Officer Welch thought he would be when he entered the police academy, thin, fit, and liked by everyone. It seemed that every time there was a shootout, Officer Wilcox was there saving the day. He'd been the hero on more than one occasion.

"Hey, Welch. I brought you a sandwich. I thought you might be hungry."

Welch got out of his seat and took the sandwich bag.

"That's really nice of you. Thanks. I'm starving."

To Officer Welch, this kind of small gesture was a big thing in the world. Maybe he should do the same for others. Pay it forward, as they say. Maybe they would look at him the same way they looked at Officer Wilcox. That altruistic thought would fade quicker than his walk down to his vehicle.

"Anything interesting happen tonight?" Wilcox asked.

"Oh, you know, this and that," Welch said, trying to sound nonchalant, but then he looked around conspiratorially and whispered, "There was a visitor from the White House. While he was here, the senator had a heart attack."

It was a little white lie, but Welch came from a long line of embellishers. It was in his nature.

"Does the chief know?" Wilcox asked.

"Sure, yeah. Everything's gonna be alright. I took care of it."

"Okay, great. Why don't you head home and get some shuteye. I'm sure you've earned it."

Welch gave a stretch and a groan that might have implied that he had just stormed Normandy and deserved a two-week R & R.

"Well, Mattie, I'll see you tomorrow, pal. And thanks again for the sandwich."

"See you tomorrow, Welch. And hey, I heard about your trip to Cancun. Sounds like you got a sweet deal."

Welch gave a meaty grin. "You got that right. It can't come soon enough." He waved a goodbye and left.

Officer Wilcox took the seat that Welch had just been occupying and flipped open a book that he had brought with him.

Maybe I should start reading too, Officer Welch thought to himself. He added it to the long list of items he meant to get around to, but deep down he knew he never would. Now he was just content to be off duty with a sandwich in hand.

———

FOWLER EXPECTED TO FEEL PAIN, BUT INSTEAD HE FELT A strange sense of euphoria. His mind floated this way and that. Snapshots of his life strode by on wooden legs. Rivers of past emotions swirled and swished, giving the senator the feel of a psychedelic out-of-body experience.

"Wake up," he told himself. "Wake up."

But the voice sounded strange. It didn't sound like his own.

"Wake up, wake up."

It definitely wasn't his voice, but he recognized it, or at least he thought he did. Slowly the euphoria slipped away. And he felt pain again, sharp and biting. What was it? It was his arm. That's when he realized his eyes were closed.

"Where am I?" he thought, or did he say it out loud?

His eyes fluttered open, sleep banished away, batted into submission by the senator's panic. He couldn't blink fast enough. He had to see. Who was it? Who was telling him to wake up? He knew, but he didn't want to know. Then he recognized the voice.

"Matthew," the senator croaked.

Matthew Wilcox, the last of his sons, stood motionless, staring down at him, although the senator could barely make out his son's outline. Unbeknownst to the patient, the IV that had been in Fowler's arm was now dangling from Matthew's hand, dripping blood onto the white sheets.

"You shouldn't be here," Fowler said.

"I hear you almost died, Dad." There was no emotion in his son's voice, no amusement in his eyes, just a cold deadness.

"It was you, wasn't it? You killed those people."

"No, Dad. *You* killed those people. Let's not forget who started all this." The senator tried to sit up. His son pushed him back down. "We had an agreement, Dad." Every time he said 'dad', it sent daggers into Fowler's heart.

"I was trying to help you."

"Oh, *you* were trying to help *me*. Then what was that little charade with Lester in Virginia?"

Fowler's eyes went wide.

His son continued. "Yeah, I heard all about it. You see, Dad, cops like to talk. When I called the Roanoke Police Department, they were more than happy to tell me that the rounds Lester had in his weapon, you know, the same weapon that was supposed to kill Stokes, the rounds were *non-lethal*. Now, I'm not a forensic investigator, but I'm pretty sure non-lethal weapons going up against a man like Stokes might not be the most effective."

"I didn't know."

"Stop lying to me."

Fowler looked up at his son. He didn't know this man. The soldier he had first met on Capitol Hill all those years ago was a model citizen, a patriot, someone to be admired and loved. This abomination was his offspring?

"What did he do to you?" Fowler asked.

For the first time in recent memory, Matthew grinned.

"You mean Nick. You think I am the way I am because of him." Matthew tossed the IV tube onto Fowler's chest and the senator felt the still-leaking fluids wet his skin. "Nick just showed me the way, Dad. You're the one that planted the seed. Sometimes we'd sit up on that mountain and guess how many kids you might have out there. I'll bet if you thought about it, you couldn't remember how many women you slept with. Well, Nick was a vicious prick, but he took a liking to me. He showed me everything, every last contract that you siphoned his way. He kept records, you know. I read every one three times. It showed me the level of corruption you were willing to stoop to. You projected one image to the American public, good ol' Senator Fowler, shining light of Wisconsin. You made me reevaluate every relationship I'd had. Then when Nick died, the only person I could trust was taken away from me. Do you understand what that feels like? You finally see the light, and then the tool of your salvation is snatched from your hands."

"That wasn't my fault. Nick was reckless. You knew that," Fowler said, trying to make his son see reason.

"I don't deny that. I was just lucky enough to be overseas when it happened, otherwise you might have lost two sons. I couldn't get to him before Stokes, but I did see them carry his body away."

"I did think I'd lost you. I told you how that crushed me."

"That's touching. It crushed you so badly that you had to go looking for your other son."

"How did you know," Fowler said quietly.

"I put it together. You showed a little bit too much defer-ence to Tommy. A strand of hair from each of you confirmed my suspicions. All it took after that was a night of hard drink-ing. It didn't take much to push him over the edge. He couldn't take it. Could you imagine not knowing who your own father was? I needed him, but he still followed through on his promises to you. He delivered the message to Stokes before I could get it. But he died hating you. And isn't that what really matters, a love between father and son?"

When Fowler had told Stokes that Matthew had killed Tommy, it had only been a guess. Here was the confirmation.

Oh God, he thought, *What have I done?*

"So here we are, Dad. We're the only ones left. But I've got a little problem and that problem is spelled D-A-D." Matthew tapped his forefinger on the top of Fowler's head as he recited each letter. "You're weak, Dad. You told me there was no room in this world for weakness. You explained how Nick's weaknesses gave Stokes the edge." He paused and stroked his father's head, brushing the hair from his eyes. "As much as your beloved Tommy would hate for me to do this, I'm going to have to say goodbye."

Matthew snatched the pillow from under Fowler's head before the senator could react. He tried to call out, but Matthew was too fast, slamming the pillow onto his face and pressing down.

God save me, Fowler thought, trying to catch his breath, trying to push his son away, trying to chew through the suffo-cating fabric. *This can't be how it ends. It can't be.*

The pressure was gone. He could breathe again. He looked up at Matthew through blurry eyes.

"I forgot one thing, Dad. Say hi to Nick for me."

Then the pillow slammed back down again. The pain blossomed in his chest and he felt his whole body go rigid. *Will my life flash before me?* Fowler thought. The pain was excruciating, spreading out to every extremity. It burned his eyes.

Then, without fighting any longer, he exhaled for the last time.

———

OFFICER WILCOX CAREFULLY UNCLIPPED THE DEVICE HE'D used to reroute the signals from the hospital monitors to Senator Fowler's body. As soon as the last lead was attached, the alarms started going off again. Unconcerned, he put the device in his pocket, knowing that the nurses and doctors would be too late. He'd waited five minutes, just to be sure.

A nurse was the first to rush in, a napkin still tucked into her scrub shirt. "What happened?"

"I don't know. The alarm went off, and I came in," Wilcox said. The nurse glanced at the monitors and down at the senator.

"Oh no, not again." She pressed a button on the wall and soon doctors flooded the room as well.

Officer Matthew Wilcox backed up to the far wall and watched it all, a look of concern stamped on his face. But in his heart, he felt nothing. In his mind, he only imagined opportunity. They worked on the senator for fifteen minutes. It was impressive. Nobody wanted him to die on their watch. But in the end, it was to no avail. United States Senator Warren Fowler died at 3:17 in the morning.

CHAPTER THIRTY-THREE

Senator Fowler was very much an unknown outside of his home state. The only reason his death got so much nationwide coverage was because his passing coincided with what was now being called a terrorist attack in a suburban Milwaukee office park. The senator's death raised the total death toll to nineteen.

That morning, when news reached citizens of Wisconsin, it triggered an outpouring of grief, culminating in thousands of mourners surrounding the hospital where the senator's body now lay. Three Boy Scout troops came, each young man reverently holding an American flag. A hundred-plus contingent of the local VFW rode in on motorcycles despite the cold. Countless local organizations who'd been touched by the senator's good work converged to get a glimpse of the place where their benefactor took his last breaths.

"I'd say we have probably about ten thousand people out there," said the television reporter. "And we've got a lot more coming. The police are telling us that the senator's body will be leaving in approximately five minutes. We're going to pause now for station identification. We'll return shortly to bring you our ongoing coverage of Terror in Wisconsin."

Daniel turned off the television and looked to the others. "Do you really think it was a heart attack?"

"He was in rough shape when I left him," Cal said. "Anything is possible."

"Is there any chance they could pin this back on you, Cal?" Top said. "I mean, you had just been there."

"I don't think so. I did wait around and make sure he made it before I left. No, I think the old man's heart gave out. I heard the doctor say he had a pre-existing condition and that the stress from the explosion made things worse."

"Well, hell. Just when we thought we were getting somewhere," Gaucho said. "Neil, have you had any luck on the name Matthew Wilcox?"

"Not really," Neil said. "There are twenty-five listings for Matthew Wilcox in the greater Milwaukee area alone. Expand the search and it just becomes more. I'd really hoped for Army records to come through."

"Yeah, me too," Cal said.

The military was usually a reliable source for personnel information, but for some reason there was no record of a Matthew Wilcox ever having served. Now, Cal and his friends would never know if it had been Senator Fowler who made his son's official military record disappear.

"If we just knew what he looked like," Gaucho said. They'd poured over the surveillance video, but none of Neil's tricks yielded a single hit. The man was a ghost. They'd discussed the conundrum, and came to the conclusion that it had probably been designed that way.

"Let's go back to what we know," Daniel said. "We know he had some kind of contact with the senator's men. Lester, you're sure you've never heard of this guy?"

"I swear."

"And what about your dad, do you think he knows him?"

Lester shrugged. "I wish I knew. I mean, for all I know, he's dead, right?"

"We don't know that yet," Daniel offered. "They're still clearing the building. Maybe he's just unconscious somewhere, lying in a hospital bed."

"Maybe," Lester said. There was only hint of sadness in his words, probably more regret than grief.

"I say we start there," Top said. "Let's find Lester's dad and see what he knows. If they haven't found him by now, I'm sure he got out."

What Cal really wanted to do was raid the senator's office and his home. But with every federal agency from the FBI on down descending on Milwaukee, that would be impossible.

"All right, let's start with Robert Howe," Cal said. "Top, Gaucho, get on the phone with the local police department. See if they have any John Does that were taken to area hospitals. Lester, you and Daniel brainstorm places where your father might be hiding."

"I can think of a couple places," Lester said.

"Good. Write them all down, starting with the most likely. I've got to call a friend and see if they won't let us in on the FBI investigation."

Everyone but Lester knew that by *friend,* Cal meant the president.

He was just going to punch into the president's secure line when the caller ID indicated that Diane was calling. For a second, he thought about sending the call to voicemail. *Bad idea,* he thought. Despite the pressing matters in Wisconsin, he still had to think of Diane. In addition to everything that had happened, he had to contend with the fact that he'd been wrong, at least partly.

He'd never agreed with fellow Marines and government workers who thought wives and families should just sit there and take it, proud of the fact that their husband served their country. That pride faded quickly when absence became the norm. Cal didn't want to be that man. He wanted a life. He wanted kids. There had to be a way to have both. Maybe just admitting it to Diane was a first step. He took a deep breath and answered the call.

"Hey, babe. I was—"

"*Cal?*" Her voice shook.

"Diane, what's wrong?" Cal felt everyone in the room freeze around him.

"*Cal, he wants to talk to you.*"

"Who?"

There was a jostling of the phone, and then a male voice said, "*Cal Stokes. How nice it is to finally speak with you.*"

The voice sent a jolt of panic through Cal's body. "*What have you done with her?*"

"*Oh, she's just fine. I must say, she is a pretty girl. We always said in the Army that Marines get the prettiest girls because of your fancy blues. But I guess we were wrong. Turns out I've got the pretty girl now.*"

"What do you want?"

"*Oh, come on now, Stokes. You're not that dense, are you? Are you one of those Marines that had to retake the entrance exam just to enlist?*"

"Now listen here, you son of a—"

"*Language, Stokes, language. Unkind words won't be necessary. Uncouth was what my mother called it.*"

Cal couldn't be sure, but he thought he heard mumbling in the background.

"*So, my father told you who I am. Don't try looking for me. It's unnecessary. You won't be able to find me. But not to worry. Keep your phone on, and I'll be in touch.*"

"How do I know that you won't hurt her?"

"*Oh, I don't know. I guess you'll just have to trust me.*"

"I swear, if you hurt her, I'll—"

"*Don't make promises you can't keep, Stokes. I'm quite sure that Miss Mayer here is quite through with your lies. Now settle down, pack your things, and I'll be in touch.*"

"Let me talk to her," but the phone call had already gone dead.

Cal's body felt like it was going to explode. It was happening again. Someone he loved was in mortal danger. He didn't even have time to place the fault on himself. His mind was already tumbling down the path of worst case scenario.

I will find you, Cal thought, unable to shake the feeling that his lies were finally coming home to roost.

CHAPTER THIRTY-FOUR

There was no time for preparation. Cal got a text from Wilcox five minutes later. An Uber would meet him at a specific intersection. He should go alone.

"You can't go by yourself," Gaucho said. "We'll follow you."

"This guy's not stupid." Cal was emptying his pockets, per the instructions that had been tagged to the end of the text. No belongings, no phone, not even a wallet.

"I am trying to trace the call from Diane's phone," Neil said, "Maybe I'll get something."

"Fine, keep working. But I need to go."

"Cal, you need to stop and think about this," Daniel said.

"No, she's in trouble and it's my fault. If I don't get there and meet that Uber, who knows what will happen. His instructions were pretty clear. Just do what you can. I need to go. Promise me you'll do everything you can for Diane."

"I promise," Daniel said, and the two men shook hands. "Be careful, Cal."

"I will."

Cal ran along the snow-lined sidewalk until he reached the

exact spot where Matthew Wilcox wanted him to be. He waited, casually looking around to see if he was being watched, but he couldn't point out any definites. There was light traffic, and any one of a handful of vehicles passing by could be running surveillance. A Dodge Caravan skidded to the curb a few minutes after Cal had arrived.

"Are you Cal?" the young man said. He sported a full beard and looked like he would have a hard time getting out from behind the wheel, his girth wedging him in like a country ham.

"I'm Cal."

"Well, hop in."

Cal got in the back, careful to buckle his seatbelt. The driver, whose name was Dallas, headed away as he followed the directions on the GPS. Cal played along, not sure if Dallas was part of Wilcox's scheme or if he was just an everyday Uber driver. He was probably the latter, as he never caught Dallas looking in the rear view unless he was asking Cal a question. Cal would answer with a yes or no or maybe an occasional grunt. If Dallas was an actor, he was very good.

Finally, Cal interrupted the ongoing monologue, "Hey, Dallas, excuse me, but where exactly are we going?"

Dallas looked up in the rear view with confusion. "You called me. Don't you know?"

"Well, it's sort of a surprise. It's my birthday and my friends are doing this weird scavenger hunt thing."

"Oh, that's cool. Man, I haven't done a scavenger hunt since I was in high school. My parents put it together and made me go all over town. It was cool because I got to bring my friends and they gave each group one of those Polaroid cameras. Every time we got somewhere and found like a statue we were supposed to take a picture with, we got to use the Polaroid camera. It was awesome. I wish I could do that again."

"Dallas," Cal interrupted. "Where are we going?"

"Well, I don't want to ruin the surprise. What fun would that be?"

Cal tried to control his breathing. "How about you give me your address, and I'll drop you fifty bucks in the mail after this is over. I'm not big on surprises."

"I'd rather take fifty bucks cash now, but ..." Dallas took a moment to decide. "Okay, sure. Left Field. I've never been there. Weird name. I'll bet some rich dude owns it, made up the name to be funny." He touched the cell phone screen and scrolled the map forward. "There, see?"

"Okay, thanks. I appreciate it."

"Yeah, no problem. So anyway, like I was saying," Dallas prattled on, and Cal only half listened, seriously considering reaching over the seat, snatching the man's phone, and calling his friends. Maybe they could get there in time. In the end, he decided against it. It was a huge risk, and he had been warned against risk taking. Multiple times.

Wilcox was proving to be a worthy adversary. If he had somehow manipulated a man like Senator Fowler, and possibly even killed him, who knew what he was capable of. Even worse, if he had been taught at the hands of Nick Ponder, Cal could envision all manner of evil tricks Wilcox might have up his sleeve.

They reached the private airfield, only after Dallas had gone into excruciating detail and relayed to Cal how difficult it was to break into a Catholic church after hours and take a Polaroid in a priest's confessional.

"Well, looks like we're here." The gate of a high fence lay open. A gravel road led inside.

It wasn't as well-cleared of snow as the main roads, but Dallas was able to maneuver the minivan onto the property, only fishtailing twice. There was no building, and no sign of human life except for a private aircraft idling on the small runway. The runway had been cleared of snow. A man stepped from the cabin as the Uber driver pulled up to the tarmac.

"Holy crap. I bet they're taking you to Vegas. Don't do any drugs when you're there, man. You seen that movie The Hangover? Scared the crap out of me. It might be funny to meet Mike Tyson, but—"

"Can you write down your address, Dallas? I want to make sure I get you that money," Cal said, wanting to get the transaction complete so he could be on the next leg of his journey.

"Sure, yeah, sorry." He took out a business card and scribbled his name and address on the back. "My address, and if you're ever in town again, feel free to call me if you need a ride."

"Thanks," Cal said, snatching the card, and leaving Dallas to his chattering.

Cal marched to the aircraft. A man who looked to be in his mid-50s was waiting.

"Mr. Stokes?"

"That's me."

"We're all set if you'd like to come inside."

"Much obliged."

The man produced a white envelope from his winter jacket. "I was told to give this to you."

Once the envelope was handed over, the man said, "I'm just going to get everything checked out and we'll be on our way. Make yourself comfortable."

Cal nodded, trying not to seem anxious. He tore open the envelope. Inside was the culmination of his worst fears: a picture of Diane, bound and gagged, staring at the camera with wide, panic-filled eyes. Cal shoved the picture in his pocket, and boarded the plane.

Other than the pilot, Cal was the only person on the private plane. Take off was smooth and uneventful, and during the flight, the only time he had any communication with the pilot was when the pilot announced they were making a stop. They made four such stops.

First, Cal assumed that they were going to refuel, but they didn't. Each time, the pilot taxied to another building, got out, and returned with another envelope. He would hand the envelope to Cal, and then lock the exterior door.

Each envelope contained a variation of the first photograph. Cal lined them up on his lap trying to discern any kind of pattern, but he couldn't find one. Wilcox was just toying with him. More breadcrumbs. But why all the stops? Why prolong the journey?

As he watched out the window, Cal could tell that they were going steadily west. Sure enough, four hours into their trip, the pilot announced over the intercom, "Mr. Stokes, we are almost to our final destination, Jackson Hole, Wyoming."

Jackson Hole. This was where it had all begun years ago. His fight with Nick Ponder, an old grudge that the vengeful Ponder just couldn't let go. He had kidnapped Neil, tortured him, and was millimeters away from concluding a successful transaction with a terrorist group when Cal and his men had swooped in.

Cal had not been back in Wyoming since. He'd lost his good friend, a Navy Corpsman named Brian Ramirez. *That damned mountain*, he thought. Cal's vision went back to that fateful day. Watching Brian wave to him from the distance. The next second, Ponder's mountaintop fortress exploded, rigged during construction by Ponder himself, should he have to escape in a hurry. His friend died and so had others, more of Cal's men. And now here he was again at the scene of the crime.

Was Wilcox bringing him here to relive those awful days? Was it more games? Were they going to touch down only to have another plane pick him up minutes later? These were all questions running through Cal's head as the pilot executed another perfect landing and taxied to a small hanger.

"The tower just radioed and said there's a car waiting for you," the pilot said, as he opened the aircraft door. "Have a nice visit."

Cal rushed out into the cold and climbed into the waiting vehicle. It was another Uber, but at least this time, the driver was a man in his sixties who barely said five words as he took the long road toward a familiar sight. It was the center of the posh Jackson Hole community. Cal could only see the bottom of the ski slope, and its revolving ski lift as they approached. Most of the mountain was obscured by clouds and falling snow. The driver dropped him off at their destination, a ski shop next to Hotel Terra, the same hotel that he had stayed in those years before when they'd gone in search of Neil. He did not receive further instructions from the driver, who pulled away as soon as Cal had closed the door. But when he looked back at the ski shop, there was a man waiting with a wide grin.

"Mr. Stokes?" he said cheerily

"That's me."

"We've got you all set up inside."

Cal followed the man into the shop. The man then pointed towards changing rooms and said, "Your friend sent over your sizes. I think everything should fit. But you might want to try them on just in case. I'll be right outside if you need me to exchange anything."

Cal did as instructed and slipped into the changing area, glancing all around to see if he was supposed to meet some- one. It was empty. He was the only patron. He went inside the first stall and found an array of ski clothing. Slick black ski pants, a bright red coat, a pair of goggles, and a Nike beanie. The only thing he had to exchange after he tried them on were the gloves.

"And now, if you'll come on out, we'll get you fitted in boots. A preference on skis?" the helpful retail clerk asked.

"Whatever my friend ordered is fine," Cal said, anxious to be on his way.

"Good choice," the young man said. "Have to say, they picked out the best for you. You must have some really great friends."

"Yeah, they're perfect." Cal said, falling far short of the other man's cheeriness.

Ten minutes later, Cal was out the door, but not before a grinning young man handed him another envelope.

"Have a great trip, and if you ever get a chance to stop by, we'd love to know how the rest of your surprises went."

Surprises. Cal knew that Wilcox would have plenty of those. He tore open the seventh envelope of the day and found a computer-printed note along with a lift ticket. The note said:

Take the lift to the top of the mountain but wait to get on at exactly 3:15.

Cal glanced at his watch. He had a good fifteen minutes. He was hungry. He could feel the unfamiliar altitude already pressing down on him. If he had had his wallet, he would've grabbed a snack and a drink, just to be prepared, but he didn't have any money.

Fourteen minutes and thirty seconds later, he was poised at the right spot. The snow was really coming down now, and he could barely see 30 feet in front of him. He timed his approach perfectly so that he would arrive at the exact moment noted in the letter. Luckily, the line was sparse and he was able to scoot in front of a family, saying that his wife was up ahead and he'd like to catch up. The family moved aside and Cal stepped into their place. Skis centered, poles in one hand, he saw the chair coming around the curb. Just before it came up from behind him, another skier swished in.

"Mind if I join you?" the man asked.

Cal had no time to respond, because the lift scooped them up and took them into the air.

"Wow, can you believe all this snow?" the man said. "Beautiful."

He was wearing goggles and a black neoprene mask that obscured his entire face.

"Yeah," was all that Cal could say.

"You look pretty tense. You should loosen up, you know. No good to ski with tight legs."

Cal ignored the comment, trying to see up ahead though the snow. It seemed to be getting worse, the higher they went.

"You know, Cal, for a guy that's supposed to be as much of a badass as you, I would've expected you to be a little more relaxed."

Cal's head snapped back to the man. It was only then that he saw the silencer-extended pistol in a gloved hand. He could've sworn the man was smiling beneath his mask.

"Don't try anything, Cal. Diane wouldn't want it."

"If you hurt her..."

"Oh, stop it, silly. You'll get to see her soon enough. I figured we could take a little trip first. Get you reacquainted with the area."

Every fiber in his body was tense and ready to strike, but Cal, not knowing whether this man was indeed Matthew Wilcox or one of his lackeys, understood that attacking the man could mean certain death for Diane.

Cal willed his body to relax and asked, "When do we get there?"

The other man draped one leg over the other, as if he was getting ready to sit back and take a quick snooze on the way up the mountain. "Don't you worry about that. Just sit back and enjoy the ride."

CHAPTER THIRTY-FIVE

"I love the snow," said the man. "If it were up to me I'd live in the snow all the time. It really separates the strong from the weak. I like that. I like the great equalizers. Water is like that too. I've never been to BUDS, but they tell me that the water and the cold is what gets most people. Can you believe that? The toughest of the tough, and a simple thing like water breaks them." He laughed. "That makes me think that Mother Earth is going to win. She's going to find out some way to get rid of us all. Until then, she's content to throw these little tests our way. A tsunami here. A snowstorm there."

"Where is Diane?" Cal said, careful to keep his voice calm.

"Oh, she's fine for now. But what happens to her is really up to you."

"Don't hurt her."

"Cal, do you really think I'd be sitting right next to you if I didn't have some contingency to kill you? How do you know those ski boots aren't rigged explosives? How do you know a sniper isn't watching us?" He pointed to the chair coming behind them. "I'm ten steps ahead of you, Cal, so you better get used to it."

"You're Wilcox, aren't you?"

The man shrugged. "Names don't mean much to me anymore."

"What do you want?"

"I told you. I want you to sit back and enjoy the ride." Just as he said it, the lift swung to a stop. "Oops. I guess this is us!"

Cal looked all around. By his estimation, they were still far from the top of the ski run.

Wilcox lifted the safety bar and pointed to the ground. "You first."

Cal couldn't see the ground. It was maybe 20-30 feet below them, but he couldn't be sure. "You're kidding right?"

"You've never been heli-skiing before? Don't worry. It's all powder down there. No trees, I promise. At least I think. You'll see the ground coming. Stay loose. Absorb the impact. I'll be right behind you."

Cal imagined getting impaled on a tree or cracking his head on a rock below, but what choice did he have? He scooted forward onto the edge of the seat, took a deep breath, and jumped.

Wilcox was right. Cal did see the ground as he fell through the snow-filled air, and thankfully, the ground was clear. His honed reflexes took the impact, but he overcompensated one way, almost tumbling downhill. He was able to jab a ski pole into the ground and stop himself from falling. Cal was up to his chest in snow. He turned to see Wilcox already on the ground, and sitting higher in the snow than he was.

"Here, put these on," Wilcox said, tossing Cal another pair of goggles. Cal slipped the old goggles off, put them in a pocket, and put on the new ones. "Push the button on the side."

Cal did as he was told, and a moment later an overlay appeared on the glass in front of his eyes, like a heads-up display in a car.

"Just follow the arrow," Wilcox instructed.

What hadn't the man thought of? With Cal being out front he was limited to what he could do. He probably couldn't outrun the man behind him. Cal was a decent skier, but he could tell that Wilcox was more than his match. Feigning injury was one option, but where would that get him? He needed to get to Diane. So after quickly checking his skis and making sure his mask fully protected him from the elements, Cal set off through the falling snow.

The GPS guided path cut them across the mountain, and gradually, Cal could feel that they were losing altitude. They didn't stop once, and Cal estimated that it had been over two hours before they got to a spot marked with an 'X' in his goggle display.

Cal stopped, looked back at Wilcox.

"See that tree right there?" Wilcox said, pointing to an enormous pine. "Look underneath and you'll find our next ride."

The snow had piled so high that it created a kind of bowl-shaped indentation under the tree where the snow hadn't fallen. Underneath Cal could barely make out two forms that stood out, but only after he'd skimmed the area three times. It was white camouflage tarping, and when he pulled one back he found a snowmobile waiting.

"Hop on," Wilcox said, clicking off his skis and mounting the second snowmobile. Cal followed suit, stacking his skis under the pine tree next to Wilcox's.

He stepped onto the snowmobile and noticed that it still

felt warm. How long ago had someone put them there? Were they watching close by?

The engine turned over and revved without effort. As soon as Cal moved forward, his heads-up display pointed the way again. No coordinates or distance measurements, just an arrow nudging them this way or that. Cal followed it again. This time they moved uphill. There was a ninety-degree turn at one point, taking them roughly back the way they'd come, farther up the mountain, farther into the drifts of snow. In a few places, Cal could have sworn that he felt snow shift below him. Were they going over a mountain face ripe for an avalanche? *Maybe I could start one*, Cal thought. But just as quickly, he threw the idea away. Any contingency he might bring to bear was trumped by the fact that Wilcox had Diane.

On and on they went, farther up the mountain. Finally they crested a ridge, and Wilcox pulled up behind him. "Home sweet home. Do you see it?" he said, pointing.

Cal squinted, but couldn't see anything through the heavy snow.

"You don't remember? Oh, well, this will be fun then. Really thought you'd figured it out." This time, Wilcox took the lead, seemingly unconcerned that Cal might try to make a move. Cal soon realized why. Maneuvering into an attack position would be impossible. The path might have been one and half times the width of the snowmobile. To make matters worse, the ledge they skirted dropped away into nothingness. Wilcox zoomed along the rim like he'd done it a thousand times. Cal was not afraid of heights, but he did have to focus on the man up ahead, careful not to skid to the right. To his left was a rock wall that would have been impossible to scale in the current condition.

They followed the tiny path, flying along at breakneck speed. Not long after, Wilcox slowed and raised his hand signaling Cal to stop. Cal was able to slow the vehicle down, but still bumped into the snowmobile in front of him. Wilcox had already jumped off and the rear end of the vehicle shifted menacingly close to the edge of the cliff. Wilcox didn't seem to notice. Either that or he didn't seem to care.

"Let's go," he said. There was plenty of room for Cal to walk around Wilcox, but instead Wilcox walked backwards, weapon leveled, always watching the approaching Marine. "The door is right there," Wilcox said, pointing to the stone wall. Sure enough, when Cal looked left, there was a door inlaid perfectly so that you could only see it if you were standing right in front of the thing. If he had been cruising along by himself on the snowmobile, he probably would have missed it. No, he *definitely* would have missed it.

"Open the door," Wilcox ordered.

Cal reached out, pulled the lever, much like the ones they have on naval warships, and the metal door creaked open. As soon as slightly warmer air hit Cal in the face, he heard it, above the wail of the wind, through the blinding snow. Screams. But not just any screams.

The screams of a woman.

CHAPTER THIRTY-SIX

Cal yelled "Diane!" before he'd even realized he'd said it. He rushed into the dark space, slipping as his ski boots hit the slick floor. He was flat on his back, having taken a nasty hit to the head. He could still hear the screams; then through it all he heard a voice call his name. It was Diane. He knew it. Cal flipped onto his stomach and pushed himself up. Wilcox was in the door, closing it. Then he flipped a switch on the wall and florescent lights flickered on overhead.

"How's your head?" he asked. "You shouldn't have rushed in like that." He said it matter-of-factly, almost like he was bored, like the show was over.

There was a small alcove at knee level to Wilcox where he pulled out a pair of boots and threw them to Cal. "Here, take a pair."

Cal caught them, and that's when he realized the screaming had stopped. He wanted to do something, do anything, throttle Wilcox, run to Diane's aid. But even as he took off his ski boots and replaced them with the rubber soled ones he'd been given, he knew he was stuck. He examined every angle. Wilcox stood there quietly, weapon ready as if to say, "Try me, cowboy."

Once Cal was finished and standing an appropriate distance away, Wilcox grabbed his own boots and slipped them on quickly. Still Cal was ready. Always watching. He never had a shot.

"Okay, let's go. Walk."

Wilcox gestured down the hallway. Motion sensor lights came to life as they moved deeper into the mountain. There were no doors, just the slick slabs of concrete on every side, moisture running down in thin streams. It was cold, though not unbearable. Wilcox still had his mask on. Cal wondered if that was just part of his shtick.

Finally they came to a door at the very end of the hallway.

"Open it," Wilcox said.

Cal grabbed the handle, twisted and pulled, a blast of warm air hit him in the face. He smelled fresh paint. He noticed a strip of blue painter's tape still fixed to a far wall. Inside, the room that was roughly rectangular and spacious. There was a row of empty bookcases, a couple of sturdy wooden folding chairs, and a desk. There was something on the desk, a clear cylindrical container, with water in it. Cal couldn't tell what it was.

"Take a seat," Wilcox said, pointing to one of the chairs. Cal grabbed the first chair and scooted it up to the desk. There was something floating in the water of the vase. He noticed now it wasn't really a vase, as it was completely enclosed. Inside it was something that looked like seaweed or floating grass.

"Put these on." Wilcox threw him a set of handcuffs. "On your wrists" he specified. Cal put them on, ratcheting down until metal touched on both sides. Wilcox produced two more sets of handcuffs and said, "Bolt each ankle to the chair." Cal complied, and was given one last set, this one with a longer chain attaching each cuff, to secure all the previous sets together.

By the time Cal was done, Wilcox was sitting in a swivel chair on the other side of the desk. "What do you think? Do you like it?"

Cal didn't answer.

"Aw, come on, Cal. Pretty impressive that we built this all the way up here. My dad spent a lot of money on it." He looked to Cal for a response. "Nothing? Well, I'll be impressed for the both of us. You can't imagine how much trouble it was. We had to use helicopters to get everything up here. Concrete, supplies, workers. But where there's a will, there's a way. Am I right? Woo, tough crowd. Fine, fine. You don't want to chat. I understand. I'd be pissed off too if I was you. I mean, in reality, I was you. Aside from not having a father while I was growing up, my life was pretty good. My mom loved me. I was a pretty smart kid. Did well in school. Went into the Army. The American dream.

"What the hell happened to you?"

"The Army changed me. Maybe it happened to you too. It taught me that *I* was the only one in charge of my destiny. If I wanted something, I had to take it. I had to work hard. I had to be a thousand percent. As long as I could sustain that, I could win. I was a good kid before that. I mean, I was a good kid in the Army too, but they raised me into a man. They taught me things I could never learn in any other school. How to shoot, how to hunt, how to become someone else."

"Why don't you take off the mask?" Cal could barely see the man's eyes through the orange tinted goggles.

"I don't think we're ready for that yet," Wilcox said, putting his hands behind his head and leaning back in his chair. "So tell me if I've got this right. Your parents die on 9/11. Instead of finishing at UVA, you enlist in the Marine Corps. You serve your time, become a big hero, earn the

Navy cross, and then you get out and work for your father's company. SSI, was it?"

Wilcox looked at Cal, but Cal said nothing.

"I'll take your silence as assent. From there things get a little hazy. You're on the rolls of The Jefferson Group, a Charlottesville-based consultancy. You're technically listed as a consultant, but you and I know that 'consultant' is pretty far from what you do, correct?"

Still no answer from Cal.

Wilcox waved his hands in the air as if he was shooing away a stupid question. "Either way, we've got a lot in common, Cal Stokes. We're both in the killing business. We both lost our parents and we both had fathers who... mmm, how shall I put this? Well, they were *liars*."

Cal sat up a little straighter. "You don't know a thing about my father."

Wilcox leaned forward and rubbed his masked chin. "You don't know, do you?"

"Know what?"

"Holy Mary, Mother of Jesus!" Wilcox said, throwing his head back in a raucous laugh. "You really don't know. Oh man, this keeps getting better and better. I swear, I wish I was videotaping your face right now."

Cal didn't know if the man was insane or if there was any merit to what he was saying, but what really got to Cal was the man's attitude. He was like an arrogant teen who thinks he can do anything he wants. Perhaps that was the case for now, but Cal still had to find a way in, some way to twist the opportunities in his direction.

"Nick, what do you think? Do you think Cal knows? Or do you think he's just pretending he doesn't know? What's that, Nick? I can't hear what you're saying."

Maybe he really is crazy, Cal thought.

"Oh, I'm sorry, you probably just think I'm babbling. Cal,

you remember Nick." Wilcox reached over to the glass container filled with clear liquid and whatever was floating around inside. He turned it around with both hands.

The features were blanched and twisted. One side of his mouth curled up in what could have been a wicked grin. There were two puncture wounds in the left cheek, bullet holes that Cal had placed there himself on a dark night in Pakistan.

It was the lifeless head of Nick Ponder.

Cal shook his head in disgust. "So is this what you do? Hide in your little hole and talk to your dead brother?"

"He's not dead, Cal. Didn't you know that? He lives on, in here." Wilcox pointed to his chest. "Nick was a vicious prick, but once he found out who I was, I was family and that was that. I knew a lot before I started working for Nick, but he taught me more. He showed me how to use the system. Taught me how to manipulate our father. I just took what Nick taught me and made it better - more streamlined, less waste. Nick drank himself to sleep. I never touch the stuff. Nick loved cheap hookers. I only date former high school prom queens. So you see, Cal, we do have a lot in common. I took over my brother's company and then my father's. You took over your father's. You date pretty girls. But let's get back to why we're really sitting here. You killed my brother. You killed the man that welcomed me with open arms when my dad cast me out like a dog."

"Why don't you just get this over with? Let Diane go and you can do whatever you want with me. I'm starting to tire of your soliloquies."

"*Tch tch*, such a histrionic little action hero, aren't you? Oh, don't you worry. I'll let her go at some point. I don't hurt women or children. It's another way that I'm very much not like my brother. But Nick respected that. He understood his flaws just like I understand my strengths. One of the things

I'm the best at is reading people. Take now, for example. You'd like nothing better than to jump over this desk and kill me with your bare hands."

"That was a tough one to figure out."

"Okay, so that was an easy one. But what I really see in your eyes is what I mentioned a minute ago. You want to know why I brought your father into this. You want to know why I called him a liar. There it is! You try to hide it" Wilcox jabbed his finger toward Cal. "I see it in your eyes. That little seed of doubt. Let me tell you about doubt, Cal. I was a bright shining star in the Army. Then I came home to find my mother dying of cancer. Stage four. Can you believe that? She'd been waiting for me to get home because she didn't want to tell me while I was fighting the goddamn Taliban. She waited to get treatment. I wasn't angry, but I'd promised her I'd be there. You know what she did just before she died? She told me my father was alive. She told me that when she was younger and a bit naïve, she'd slept with a certain gentlemen and that rendezvous had resulted in my birth. She then went on to tell me that the gentlemen happened to be a certain senator from Wisconsin. You'd have thought I'd been mad, but I wasn't. I never had a dad like you did. So I pulled some strings. I found out that he was looking for a military aide, and the Army sent me to his office. I had to give it to him. He handled it pretty well when I told him. He didn't seem too surprised. He agreed to bring me on. I never asked him for anything. I just told him that I wanted to get to know him.

"Those first days we did get to know one another. We spent time together, shared meals. He asked me about my life, and told me about his. But then something happened, and as I look back, I know it was only natural. It was doubt, Cal. Not from me. I didn't have a doubt that this was my father. I believed my mother, but the senator wanted me to get a DNA test. He wanted to make sure I was his son. I refused. He'd already admitted to sleeping with my mother and the timelines all worked out, so why get a test? Why not just go on faith? But he pushed and pushed and all I could think about was, is this the way a father treats a son? So I quit. I left, but not before discovering that the vaunted Senator Warren Fowler had another son, Nick Ponder. It took me a while to track good ol' Nick down, but when I did, well, my life changed. I won't go into all the details, because they don't really matter. And at any rate, you know what happened in the end. Nick got careless and you took care of him. And that's fine, really. Honestly, if it were just about Nick, I might not even care. Sure, he was my brother, and sure, I should feel some kind of anger towards you for killing him, but if there was one thing that I learned from Nick and my father, it was that business comes first. That is where you and I have a problem. You know I exist, and while this might seem like the start of a wonderful tale of good versus evil, that's not what it's going to be. With the help of my father, I've erased every shred of evidence that I ever existed. My Army records, gone. My Milwaukee Police Department records, vanished. *Poof.*"

"So why are you still talking? Why don't you just kill me?"

"I'll admit, I'm a little theatrical. I hope you can excuse that. I'm pretty straight-laced when it comes to most things, but I can't really share this with anyone else. I wanted you to be here for the birth, or maybe it should be called the rebirth, of my life. With your death comes my transformation. I kind of like that. Like a black butterfly coming out of a cocoon." Wilcox looked up at the ceiling as if he was picturing it. "Well anyway, I wanted you to be here for it." Wilcox clapped his hands together and jumped to his feet. "I'm tired of talking."

As Wilcox walked around the desk, Cal thought he was going to uncuff him. Instead, he grabbed the back of the wooden chair, dragged to the far end of the room, the wooden legs screeching along the concrete floor. Then he pushed one of the empty bookcases to the side. The bookcase was on some kind of rail system, and when it was moved, a door was revealed. Cal could just see it as he craned his neck to look behind him.

The door opened, and Diane's screams filled the room.

"Where do women learn how to scream like that?" Wilcox said to no one in particular. "I swear if they could bottle that up and make it into a weapon, yeesh." More lights clicked on as Cal was dragged from the room. "She's going to be really happy to see you, you know. You're all she talks about, Cal this and Cal that. Save Cal. Don't kill Cal. Take me instead. Blah-blah-blah. God, I love women, but really, some of them won't shut up."

Now Cal struggled to get free, but as he pulled on his bonds and started thrashing back and forth, Wilcox screamed, "Shut up!"

Diane's yelling stopped.

"Hoo, that's better. And here we are."

Wilcox swiveled around an open doorway. Cal tried to see where they were going. He could barely make a figure sitting in a matching wooden chair.

"Diane?"

"Cal?"

"Everything's going to be okay, it's—"

"Will both of you *please* shut up."

"I swear, Wilcox, if you don't let her go—"

Stars exploded in Cal's brain as Wilcox hammered him right in the temple with the butt of his pistol.

"I told you to shut up. You might not believe me, but I actually despise torture. So do me a favor and keep your trap shut."

Diane was whimpering as Wilcox set Cal's chair down and

turned him to face her. Cal saw two Dianes through his wobbly vision. He tried shaking his head to clear it.

The room smelled of sweat and fear. Diane had been crying. When he could finally focus, Cal was happy to see the anger in Diane's eyes, anger that was focused directly at Matthew Wilcox.

"So there we go. I kept my end of the bargain. You may each say your goodbyes or I love yous or whatever sentimental garbage you want to say. You've got thirty seconds."

"Diane, I love you," Cal said. "I'm sorry this happened."

"It's okay. I'm fine. He didn't hurt me," Diane said, her voice hoarse from screaming.

"See? I told you I wouldn't hurt her. Well now, I'm sorry we've got to cut this short because I've got places to be." He walked behind Diane and grabbed the back of her chair. "You are coming with me, and you, Calvin, will be staying here. I'll be right back to kill you."

"No!" Diane screamed.

"*Shhhh*" said Wilcox, the silencer pressed to his lips. "I could shoot him in both legs and let him bleed out, but that wouldn't be any fun. Besides, I'm not a monster. What kind of man would I be if the last image you had of your boyfriend was him getting his brains blown out?" They were at the door now. Wilcox pulled Diane out and then came back in the room. "You know what? I've changed my mind. I'm going to let you live." He pulled a handcuff key from his pocket and threw it into a far corner. Then he reached into another pocket, and pulled out a clear Nalgene bottle. It was three-quarters full of water. Wilcox tossed it into the same corner as the key. "If I had a Power Bar or a stick of chocolate I'd leave it for you, but that's all I've got. Sorry."

"Wait!" Cal said. "What are you doing?"

"I'm letting you live. If you can get out, then I'll be happy to see you on the outside, but I will tell you that these are steel reinforced walls. And this door, well, unless you've got the world's largest blow torch down your pants, it might be a little tough to get through. But hey, you're a Marine. You can figure it out, right?"

"You son of a—"

"Nah uh, what did I say about the language? You want her to remember the happy times, don't you? Anyhow, I'm sorry I talk so much. I usually don't talk as much, but the circumstances got me a little excited. It was great to meet you. I'm sorry we'll never talk again, but I will say that I enjoyed our journey up here." Wilcox spun on his heels, but then he stopped at the door and snapped his fingers. "Damn, I almost forgot." He spun back around and pulled another white envelope from yet another pocket. "You wanted to know about your dad. I said he was a liar." Wilcox flicked the envelope and it landed at Cal's feet. "Everything you want to know is right there. At least you'll die knowing the truth, right?"

This time Wilcox left for good. Moments after the steel door clanged shut, Cal heard Diane scream his name.

CHAPTER THIRTY-SEVEN

"It's been almost two weeks," Gaucho said, rubbing his hands over the portable stove that was propped up in the middle of the four-man tent.

"Twelve days," Daniel corrected. The blonde man's beard was coming in thick. Shaving was the least of their worries ever since they'd gotten the call from Diane. She'd been dropped by Wilcox, blindfolded, in the middle of Teton Village. A select group of Jefferson Group warriors augmented by men from SSI had arrived dressed as civilians, packing enough heat to take down a battalion. They'd gone to the obvious place first, Ponder's old headquarters on Battle-ship Mountain. According to Diane's descriptions, it should have been a perfect match, but when they arrived, the place was still in ruins. It took a whole day of hauling away rubble just to get inside. Then, just when they thought they found the corridor Diane had described, their hopes were dashed. The place was devoid of life.

That was three days into their search. From there, they'd scoured the mountain range.

And now it was day twelve.

"Do you think Wilcox came back and killed him?" Gaucho asked.

"No," Daniel said. "He's still alive."

It had been Daniel who'd led the rescue mission. Something in his eyes told the rest of them that this was how it was going to be. Of course they all trusted him, so he planned and patrolled coordinating day and night, barely getting any rest. But while Gaucho sat shivering in the tent, dreading his next turn on the mountain, Daniel looked well-rested, clear-headed, ready to hit the trail again.

The elements and time were working against them. Snow had continued to fall. Gaucho had heard the grumbles of lost hope from the other men. President Zimmer knew the situation and had offered to send troops himself, but Daniel had declined, noting that an official expedition might light up someone's radar. That would have been the last thing that Cal wanted. Senator Fowler was dead. His bastard son Matthew Wilcox had disappeared. And the federal government was still trying to explain to the public what had happened in Wisconsin. The president had enough to contend with.

"How long do we look?" Gaucho said, sounding as if he'd been afraid to ask the question. He knew, as everyone did, that Daniel, unchecked, would stay up there for the rest of his life if he believed Cal was still alive.

Neil was scouring every CCTV link he could bust into just to get a glimpse of Cal. It was possible that he could have been snuck out, but they found that option highly unlikely. Then there was the search for Wilcox himself. A man without a face. A man who no longer had a name. Neil had taken to calling him The Ghost.

"He's still alive, Gaucho," Daniel said again. "And we're gonna find him."

"How do you know?"

"I just do. Have faith, my friend."

Gaucho nodded, but had a hard time believing. He was a realist, and while he believed in the Divine, he did not hold the same type of faith that Daniel Briggs did. To add to his misgivings, Gaucho did not believe that Wilcox would have left Cal alive. Gaucho had half-expected an ambush when they arrived on the mountain, but none had come. Other than the occasional civilian explorer, they had encountered no one.

"Why don't you take a rest?" Gaucho said. "I'll wake you up when it's time for us to go."

"No. I've got a couple of places I want to look. I'll be back in an hour."

There are always places to look, Gaucho thought, shaking his head as Daniel left the tent. *Too many places.*

He guessed that, whether it was on skis or on snowmobile, Daniel had logged hundreds of miles in the past few days. How many more miles would be trudged before they would call it off? All Gaucho could do was hope that Daniel was right, and that the heart of Cal Stokes was still beating somewhere on this earth.

———

TWO WEEKS LATER, DANIEL SAT ALONE ON THE TOP OF Battleship Mountain. The men from SSI had left days before, recalled for some mission overseas. Daniel finally sent the Jefferson Group contingent minus Top and Gaucho, who refused to leave, back down the mountain to recuperate for a couple days. Daniel still felt in his heart that Cal was alive. He didn't know how, but he learned long ago not to look for an explanation, just feel it in your gut and look for the signs.

So that's what he had done. Twenty nine days they'd searched high and low, poking through snow drifts and braving sub-zero temperatures. They hunkered down at night so they could work throughout the day.

Daniel breathed in the frigid air and closed his eyes. Even though he hadn't found his friend, he felt alive and one with this place. Maybe it was being away from civilization, the fact that it was easy to lose himself in the solitude of the mountain; or maybe it was that Daniel felt the weather breaking, finally, a respite from the near-constant snowfall and howling winds.

When he opened his eyes, the clouds above parted, and a single stream of sunlight pierced through. Daniel watched as the single ray became three, four, and then too many beams of light to count. Then it was as if the veil of clouds had been lifted by God himself, leaving a clear sunny day on top of the frigid mountain.

For some reason, Daniel turned. He would never know why. In that moment, he understood. Something pulled him, beckoned him with a quiet call. And so Daniel, without question, strapped on his skis and followed the whisper on the wind.

CHAPTER THIRTY-EIGHT

*L*iar.

The word echoed inside Cal's head like a tennis ball ricocheting endlessly inside an aluminum trashcan.

He'd lost all track of time. He could feel that his body was beginning to fade, possibly its final descent. The bottle of water was long gone. As he did every time thirst overwhelmed him, he dragged his body over to lap up the minuscule droplets of moisture that ran down the walls of his cell. Down the length of the wall he worked, slowly, his tongue raw and swollen from weeks of abuse. He couldn't remember the last time he'd had to relieve himself.

For the first day, or maybe two, he had tried to find a way out. Unshackled from his chair, he tore the chair apart trying to wedge a sharp end into the door to get it off its hinges. It was impossible. Wilcox had been right. The thing weighed a ton and was as solid as a bank vault door. Next, he'd gone at concrete walls, scraping them with everything he could think of, but it was no use. He couldn't get out without help.

Wilcox was full of it. He was a sadist just like his brother.

He'd meant for Cal to suffer a long, painful death of starvation.

As hours and days drifted by, his body ate its stores of fat and muscle. His weight wasted away. He began to have vivid daydreams. Images of Diane. First, she was in bed, then walking on the beach on the Florida Panhandle, and then her ghostly figure drifted to the first time he had met her in Maury Hall at the University of Virginia. She'd challenged him that day, and he replayed the back and forth over and over and over again like his own personal movie studio inside his dreary mountain cave. But it was just a distraction. Every time he lost focus, his mind would drift back to the envelope and its contents: an old military record.

Cal now understood the doubts that Matthew Wilcox foretold. It was like a seed, which once planted, grew into a monstrous tree that sucked all life from the world. If he had been rescued within days, that tree might not have grown past the size of a sapling. The days of hunger and thirst only fed the tree, the bitterness and despair seeping into his veins.

"You were a liar," Cal said to the wavering image of his father standing before him. "You were a liar and a cheat."

His father never said a word, only stood there, staring.

"Why did you do it?" he screamed, raw tears on his cheeks. "Did mom know?"

But of course she had known. His father had stood trial. It was impossible for his mother not to know.

Infidelity. Conduct unbecoming.

Cal had read and reread the judge advocate's summary. Colonel Calvin Stokes had been accused by one of his peers of falling into the arms of a married woman while on deployment. The Jag listed the details, including times and places, as if someone had been watching his father, detailing every indiscretion. In the end, the case had been dismissed. His father had not been relieved of command. The report said there was a lack of evidence and that the credibility of the accuser was held in question. So really, it could all be a lie.

But the tree of doubt had cast its shadow, fully engulfing the shining example of his father, his hero, his friend.

With no one to talk to except for the wavering image of his father in his moments of hallucination, Cal could only go deeper and deeper, examining the case, coming up with reasons why his father might do such a thing. And then thinking what his mother must have felt when she found out. And then trying to figure out why he'd never known. Why hadn't he sensed it? Shouldn't such a thing be obvious? Sure, he had been barely a teen at the time, but surely he should've known. He could have done something!

Some days he cried, and other days he pounded the pavement until his hands were bloody and swollen. And then, an even more insidious doubt crept into Cal's mind, like a centipede nibbling its way into his brain and latching on. He started to doubt *himself*. He started to believe that his father's weakness was *his* weakness. He would never be good enough for someone like Diane. He never had a chance. He was destined to be alone. He had already lost Jessica, and it was his fault. Now he would lose Diane. And even though it might not have been through direct fault of his own, Cal didn't see it that way. He sifted through every mistake and misdeed of his life, like a judge sorting through every defendant he'd presided over in his career.

And so it was that when the door of his cell creaked opened, Cal didn't even hear it. He was looking straight at it and nothing registered. The air changed. Someone stepped inside. Cal stared, thinking it was yet another illusion, a mirage that would dash his hopes again.

The person said softly, "Cal."

He blinked once, and then again, but said nothing.

"Cal?"

Cal shook his head, but it hurt to move. "Go away. Leave me alone. I don't want to see you anymore." He couldn't know that his voice was barely a whisper. It was his father. It had to be. But why was he talking now? "Leave me alone."

The figure drifted closer. "Cal, it's okay."

"No, I said go away. I don't want to see you." The anger was welling up now. Somehow, despite the fact that he hadn't left the floor in days, Cal got to his knees and lunged at the figure, grabbing it by its throat. Even in his delirium, he was sure he would fall right through the apparition. It was just a figment of his addled mind, his father haunting him, a fragment of his doubt...

Whatever it was, it was *solid*.

"Cal, it's me, Daniel."

"Daniel?" He still couldn't see, and he wasn't sure if it was tears in his eyes or had he finally lost his vision. He thought he saw a shock of yellow.

Daniel. Daniel had blonde hair.

"Daniel?"

"It's me, Cal. It's okay. The others are coming. We're going to get you home."

"But... my dad."

"What about your dad?"

"Papers."

"Here, have some water, you look like you need it."

"No... papers. Get papers."

"There's some papers on the ground. Is that what you want me to get?"

Cal nodded, but it was his body that failed him now. "I'm sorry," he said, fuzzy edges of darkness closing in. "I'm so sorry."

As he faded away, he heard Daniel's voice, muffled by fog. "It's time to go home."

But there was no home. Not now. Not ever.

And then his world vanished.

CHAPTER THIRTY-NINE

"How's he doing?" President Zimmer asked Daniel. They were gathered in a private waiting area at Saint John's Hospital in Jackson, Wyoming. The president had just arrived.

"He's lost a lot of weight," Daniel said, "but the doc says he'll pull through."

The president shook his head slowly. "Twenty nine days. How is that even possible?"

"Ghandi survived almost that long on sips of water, and he was way older. Luckily, Cal had water. It wasn't much, but the doctor thinks that that's what kept his body going."

"That and a boatload of 'Marines never quit'," Top said. No one laughed.

Daniel had told the others what had happened in the cell. Everything that Cal had said. They'd all seen the court martial summary.

"Poor bastard," Top said. "Locked up there for a month with only his demons to keep him company."

They all stood silent for a moment, and then Daniel said, "Would you like to see him?"

Zimmer nodded.

The president was not prepared for what his eyes now beheld. Cal's once strong jawline and muscular physique were completely wasted away. It reminded the president of horrible atrocities of the world's past. How had he survived?

Diane looked up when the others entered. "Oh, Mr. President, I didn't know—"

"Diane, please. It's Brandon." He went to her and hugged her. "I'm so sorry for everything." She was a strong woman. Zimmer knew that. She did not cry. She probably cried it all out by now. "Daniel says he's gonna be okay."

Diane nodded.

"And how are you? Is there anything I can do for you?"

"No Mr.—, I mean, Brandon. I'll be fine."

But there was something else in the way Diane looked at him. Like she wanted to say something else, but was holding back. Maybe he was reading too much into it. She was dealing with Cal's imprisonment, like the others were, just in her own way. She loved him, and he undoubtedly loved her.

"Tell you what. Why don't I have my agents go out and get us some food. I'll hang out for the day, if that's okay with you."

"Yes, of course. That would be fine," Diane said. And there it was again. That look. But this time, it was furtive, like she wanted to leave, to run from the place with all haste.

Zimmer looked back down at Cal, whose emaciated face was now sucking in lungfuls of purified oxygen.

Later, as they were enjoying assortment of food brought by the president's security detail, Zimmer let them in on what the FBI had found.

"Nick Ponder was like an open book. They have a treasure trove on him. Fowler kept things guarded, but they still found handwritten notes, plus emails to Tommy Quinn. Unfortunately, there was nothing that might link him to Wilcox." He paused to stab another piece of steak and stick it into his mouth. "Wilcox is a ghost. Homeland Security, CIA, FBI, nobody knows who he is. We're trying to figure out how his files were wiped, because in this day and age, that's impossible."

They all digested the news along with their food.

"We all thought he wanted to kill Cal," Top said. "That's the information we had."

"Then why let him live?" asked Zimmer.

"If you call that living..." Gaucho said. He didn't get to finish his line because the doctor walked in.

"Your friend just regained consciousness. If you'd like to go in, you can, two at a time."

"Daniel, why don't you and the president go first?" Top suggested.

"Are you sure? You've been—" Zimmer started.

"No. You should go."

The doctor led the way, showing the two men into Cal's room.

Diane was standing over Cal, crying. She looked up when the others entered the room. "You have to talk to him. You have to."

Cal shook his head, but the president could see that it took a lot of effort to do so. Cal's lips were moving so Zimmer moved closer.

"What did you say?" the president asked.

"Tell her to go," Cal whispered.

"Tell her to go? Go where?"

"Home." Cal closed his eyes for a second, as if pushing away some hidden pain. He turned back to Diane. "Go home. I'm no good for you."

"Yes, you are. You're the one I want. Forget about everything I said before. I love you, Cal. I want to spend the rest of my life with you. And I'm not leaving this room until you leave with me."

Cal shook his head again. "You have to go."

"He's delirious," Diane said. "He doesn't know what he's saying. Doctor, what's wrong with him?"

"Severe dehydration. It's been known to cause delirium."

He stopped talking when Cal's hand reached up and touched Diane's face tenderly.

"I don't deserve you," Cal said softly. "I love you. But I don't deserve you. You have to go. Live your life."

"No, I won't go."

"Please. Go." And then his hand lowered, and he looked away from her, closing his eyes.

A single tear dropped down Cal's face and disappeared into the pillow. Zimmer stepped up to put his arm around Diane. "Why don't you go get some sleep? I'm sure he'll change his mind when he gets better."

Even as he said it, Zimmer had a sinking feeling that Cal had already set his path, that the decision had been made. His month-long confinement had locked in his speed and course. And knowing Cal Stokes, his end goal would not change. Zimmer escorted Diane from the room, all the while praying that his assumption was wrong.

EPILOGUE

It was Cal's first day back to Jefferson Group Headquarters. Almost a month had passed, but he still felt weak, and each step rattled his aching joints. But he was happy to be out of the hospital. He was unplugged from the IVs, and away from the constant poking and prodding of the hospital staff. When he entered the War Room, everyone stood and gave him a round of applause. He gave a slight bow, found a seat, and surveyed the room.

The entire headquarters staff was there, including Jonas, Dr. Higgins and the three who had spent weeks combing the Wyoming mountainside. Everyone except...

"Where's Neil?"

"He's on his way," Top said. "He's got a surprise for you."

"I'd kill for a beer right now."

It wasn't a beer that Neil brought. Preceding him into the room, with a tail wagging as quick as a hummingbird, was Liberty. She ran up to him and nuzzled her face in his hands, her tail wagging like it had fresh batteries installed.

"Hey, girl!" Cal said, stroking her brown coat and then

looking up at Daniel. "You didn't tell me she was coming home."

"They said she could do the rest of her rehab here. We thought it might be a nice welcome home gift."

"It looks like we'll be rehabbing together, girl," Cal said, bending over and kissing the dog's snout. "And speaking of rehab, how's Corporal Edgerton?"

"I put in a call to the commandant. The general said it shouldn't be problem putting him on active duty," Daniel said. "The mighty corporal says he needs time to think about it."

"Oh?"

"I think he enjoyed playing James Bond," Top said. "I wouldn't be surprised to find him on the front stoop one of these mornings. Between you me and the lamp post, Cal, I think you should give him a shot."

That made Cal smile. "I'll think about it. Now, should we get to it?"

Daniel nodded and found a seat.

Now that everyone was assembled, and Liberty was at her customary spot beside Cal, the door to the War Room was closed. Time for business.

Almost.

"Cal," Gaucho said, "Diane called. She wanted to see how you were feeling."

"How is she?" Cal asked, keeping his attention on Liberty.

"She's good. She got assigned to an intelligence outfit in Bahrain. Got there a couple days ago."

"Good for her," he said, his voice flat. "I'm sure she'll do well."

Daniel's voice broke in. "Neil, what about Wilcox? Any leads?"

Neil shook his head. "Same as yesterday. The ghost has

either buried himself in the deepest hole in the world, or he's really good at staying invisible."

"What about Brandon?" Cal said. "What's his take?"

"He's all for us looking passively," Top said. He glanced over at Gaucho, who finished for him.

"We got benched," Gaucho said.

"I can't say I'm surprised. What about the Quinns? What have you told them?"

"We wanted to wait on you for that," Daniel said.

"Good. My vote is we don't tell them anything. Mr. Quinn doesn't need to know that his wife screwed around with a senator."

"Cal," Neil started.

Cal put up his hand. "That's my decision. Now, here's what I want. We are going to get Tommy a full burial at Arlington. Daniel, can you see to it? Okay, next order of business. Me. I'm sure you guys have been sitting around worrying about me day and night. Either that or you were all fighting over my possessions. But either way, I'm going to be fine. I feel good. I feel a little like I went a blindfolded twelve rounds with Mike Tyson, but I'm okay. The plus side is I can finally eat anything I want. I'm on the mend. Nothing to it. I wanted you to hear that from me. Doc, do you agree?"

Everyone looked at Higgins. "In my professional opinion, if young Calvin sticks to the regimen provided by his doctors and continues to eat double doubles and drink milkshakes to his heart's content, we will once again have the proud Marine we once knew."

Cal waved his thanks.

"Okay, I've had a lot of time to think about this. I know you said that the president stuck us on the sidelines, but—"

A phone rang in the corner. Not just any phone, *the* phone. Its distinct ring made everyone sit up. The direct line to the president. Daniel walked over and picked up the receiver.

"This is Daniel." He nodded a couple of times and then said, "Okay, we'll call you back."

"That was quick," Cal said. "What did he want?"

As usual, Daniel did everything with as few words as possible. He walked over to the nearest computer and took it out of sleep mode. A few clicks later, he had the company email open. Cal scooted his chair closer as Daniel clicked on a file.

Daniel said, "The Russian ambassador was killed. Shot by a man as he was leaving a dinner party in Moscow."

"Holy crap. What does that have to do with us?"

Another click. A video feed popped up. It was from someone's cell phone. The men of The Jefferson Group watched as the hulking Russian ambassador stepped out of the restaurant and was immediately accosted by fans clamoring for his autograph. The ambassador smiled and took the pen from the first young woman who'd approached. That was when a vaguely familiar form stepped out of the crowd, stepped up to the Russian ambassador as if getting in line for his signature too, and shot the man in the head.

It was done so quickly, without any effort, that security took too long to react. The camera was still rolling as the assassin turned his weapon on the bodyguards, shooting them all. It took less than five seconds.

Then, the man who'd just killed four men on the streets of Moscow, looked straight at the camera and smiled.

There was a problem. The face of the man on screen was the face of one of the men in the War Room. It was the face of Cal Stokes.

———

I hope you enjoyed this story.
If you did, please take a moment to write a review <u>on Amazon.</u> Even the short ones help!

Want to stay in the loop?
Sign Up to be the FIRST to learn about new releases.
Plus get newsletter only bonus content for FREE.
Visit cg-cooper.com for details.

A portion of all profits from the sale of my novels goes to fund OPERATION C4, our nonprofit initiative serving young military officers. For more information visit OperationC4.com.

ALSO BY C. G. COOPER

The Corps Justice Series In Order:

Corps Justice (Previously Titled "Back to War")

Council Of Patriots

Prime Asset

Presidential Shift

National Burden

Lethal Misconduct

Moral Imperative

Disavowed

Chain Of Command

Papal Justice

The Zimmer Doctrine

Sabotage

Liberty Down

Sins Of The Father

A Darker Path

The Man From Belarus

Matters of State

Corps Justice Short Stories:

Chosen

God-Speed

Running

The Daniel Briggs Novels:

Adrift

Fallen

Broken

Tested

The Tom Greer Novels

A Life Worth Taking

Blood of My Kin

Stand Alone Novels

To Live

The Warden's Son

The Interrogators

Higgins

The Patriot Protocol Series:

The Patriot Protocol

The Chronicles of Benjamin Dragon:

Benjamin Dragon – Awakening

Benjamin Dragon – Legacy

Benjamin Dragon - Genesis

ABOUT THE AUTHOR

C. G. Cooper is the USA TODAY and AMAZON BESTSELLING author of the CORPS JUSTICE novels, several spinoffs and a growing number of stand-alone novels.

One of his novels, CHAIN OF COMMAND, won the 2020 James Webb Award presented by the Marine Heritage Foundation for its portrayal of the United States Marine Corps in fiction. Cooper doesn't chase awards, but this one was special.

Cooper grew up in a Navy family and traveled from one Naval base to another as he fed his love of books and a fledgling desire to write.

Upon graduating from the University of Virginia with a degree in Foreign Affairs, Cooper was commissioned in the

United States Marine Corps and went on to serve six years as an infantry officer. C. G. Cooper's final Marine duty station was in Nashville, Tennessee, where he fell in love with the laid-back lifestyle of Music City.

His first published novel, BACK TO WAR, came out of a need to link back to his time in the Marine Corps. That novel, written as a side project, spawned many follow-on novels, several exciting spinoffs, and catapulted Cooper's career.

Cooper lives just south of Nashville with his wife, three children, and their German shorthaired pointer, Liberty, who's become a popular character in the Corps Justice novels.

When he's not writing or hosting his podcast, Books In 30, Cooper spends time with his family, does his best to improve his golf handicap, and loves to shed light on the ongoing fight of everyday heroes.

Cooper loves hearing from readers and responds to every email personally.
To connect with C. G. Cooper visit
www.cg-cooper.com

ACKNOWLEDGMENTS

Another huge thanks to my Beta team members: Melissa, Kim, Glenda, Cheryl, Andy, Kathryn, Larry, Phil, Pam, Susan, Alex, John, CaryLory, Julie, Don, Bob, David, Craig, Anne & Nancy. Thanks for never giving up on me...

Made in United States
Orlando, FL
14 April 2022

16838045R00136